The Woodland Wonders

By Vera M. Roberts..

Order this book online at www.trafford.com/06-2012
or email orders@trafford.com

Most Trafford titles are also available at major online book retailers.

Note for Librarians: A cataloguing record for this book is available from Library
and Archives Canada at www.collectionscanada.ca/amicus/index-e.html

Printed in Victoria, BC, Canada.

ISBN: 978-1-4251-0255-5

*We at Trafford believe that it is the responsibility of us all, as both individuals and corporations,
to make choices that are environmentally and socially sound. You, in turn, are supporting this
responsible conduct each time you purchase a Trafford book, or make use of our publishing services.
To find out how you are helping, please visit www.trafford.com/responsiblepublishing.html*

*Our mission is to efficiently provide the world's finest, most comprehensive book publishing
service, enabling every author to experience success. To find out how to publish your book, your
way, and have it available worldwide, visit us online at www.trafford.com/10510*

 www.trafford.com

North America & international
toll-free: 1 888 232 4444 (USA & Canada)
phone: 250 383 6864 ♦ fax: 250 383 6804 ♦ email: info@trafford.com

The United Kingdom & Europe
phone: +44 (0)1865 722 113 ♦ local rate: 0845 230 9601
facsimile: +44 (0)1865 722 868 ♦ email: info.uk@trafford.com

10 9 8 7 6 5 4 3

Acknowledgment

l wish to take this opportunity to express my gratitude to:

Mrs. Maureen Plowman. Tutor of English Literature and Creative Writing

University of Wales, Cardiff.

For her support as l worked to gain the Certificate of Advanced Studies in Creative Writing.

Maureen has been my friend and mentor for many years. She is the proof reader of this book and

has given me advise and much encouragement towards achieving the University of Wales Diploma.

-:-

Dedication.

l dedicate this book to my children - the inspiration for four characters in the book:

My eldest son Paul: Who retained his title as Welsh Judo Champion for 3 years - but almost lost a

leg after two operations when he contracted gangrene: Characterizes Pogo - the kind, caring, one

legged Scarecrow.

-:-

Andrew BSc(Hons), CEng, MIStructE: who from birth fought serious disability and became a

director of an international engineering company, he worked in Europe, Oman, Hong Kong and

Tokyo overseeing construction work. Aged thirty-six he almost died in a road accident – his body

kept ice cold while recovering in the intensive care unit: Characterized as the Snowman.

-:-

Gaynor Longmuir (nee Roberts) Board member of the largest furniture company in Wales. Who at

the age of nine,was singled out from a cast of over two hundred in a news report, as the actress that

could have won an award for her performance, when she danced the part of The Little Mermaid:

Characterized as the Mermaid.

-:-

Dawn B Ed(Hons) Special Needs Teacher, who asked me to write poems and stories for her class.

As a child, she missed her brothers and sister when they married - so bought a miniature , Dutch

white rabbit for company and named it Lucky, creating the principal characters: Sally and Hop-pity.

-:-

INDEX

-:-:-

THE LITTLE WHITE RABBIT.

A little white rabbit alone in its cage sat up smartly, hoping that a lady who had entered the pet shop would notice him. She glanced down at the puppies, then picked up a kitten and began stroking it as she walked across to a large tank full of fish.

The kitten's eyes flashed excitedly watching the fish darting about in the water, then it struggled, reached out its paw and extended its sharp claws.

"Oh no you don't!" cried the lady, but the kitten fidgeted in her arms trying to get at the fish until she suddenly gave a yell as the kitten scratched her hand.

"That will never do!" she shouted crossly, hurriedly returning the kitten to a large basket where it curled up again with the others as the shopkeeper hurried across.

"Are you alright or would you like a plaster?" he enquired.

" We use blue ones at work," she smiled, catching sight of the brown rabbits cage.

The tiny white rabbit began hopping about, then he pushed his pink twitchy nose through the bars of his cage trying to draw her attention. But the brown rabbits were having so much fun the lady couldn't take her eyes off them.

"I'll buy one of these rabbits! Much safer, don't you think?"

"Definitely, Madam, they make fine pets. Rabbits are cuddly - unlike some cats!" replied the shopkeeper. "No need to walk them like dogs, just let your rabbit out of its hutch occasionally for exercise - and living in the garden it won't mess up the house!"

"That's true. I'll take that one. He seems to be enjoying himself, doesn't he?"

"He certainly does," replied the shopkeeper, unlocking the brown rabbits cage.

The lady glanced up to see a big tear rolling down the little white rabbit's face and watched it splash onto the straw in his cage.

"Look at that," she said, watching him wipe a second tear away with his paw.

"If he's got a cold it could spread to the rest of the pets."

"I don't like putting the pets in my back room, they're happier watching what's going on in the shop and listening to the birds chirping away. But I must admit he doesn't look very well.

"He's a miniature breed from Holland. I'm very particular about any stock from abroad so I've given him a thorough check every day since he arrived. He was well enough this morning but one can't be too careful! I'm sorry little rabbit you'll have to go in the back room until you're well again," said the shopkeeper.

I don't want to go in the back room, thought the little white rabbit, as he stopped crying and leaned his head to one side.

"Perhaps he's lonely being so far from home. I'd take him if he were well, my niece would love him!" remarked the lady.

Hearing those words the little white rabbit became very excited and went hopping around his cage to prove that he was definitely not ill!

"He looks fine now," said the lady, " do you think he understood what I said?"

"Of cause not, he only arrived from Holland last week, so couldn't have learnt English yet!" joked the shopkeeper. The lady laughed.

" He's lovely, I think I'll take him instead, " she smiled.

The shopkeeper put the little white rabbit into a large cardboard box and carried it to the counter.

The lady glanced up at the clock hanging on the wall

" Good gracious, I'll have to call the hospital," she said, paying the shopkeeper,

" Will it be okay if I call back for the rabbit at about four o'clock?" she asked,

The shopkeeper nodded, and the lady took a mobile phone from her handbag as she walk towards the door

" May be late! Parking ticket ran out. I was held up by a traffic warden.

Have to get away by reversing. Dr. White, " she explained, and slipped the phone

back into her bag, before she rushed off, slamming the door behind her.

The shopkeeper, put a large lettuce leaf into the box, sealed it and talked to the

little white rabbit who was looking out through a hole in the side,

" I think I'll put the hour back now, and have the day off tomorrow."

Reaching up, he took hold of his new wall clock, placed its carefully face down on

the rabbit's box and pressed a key. " I wish I could turn back time; everyone's in such

a rush these days," he said, looking at a build up of holiday traffic through the shop

window - and realised he must tend the pets if he were to have Easter Saturday off.

Leaving the clock on the box he went to get water, then picked the clock up on his

return, only to see its hand whizzing in an anticlockwise direction. Suddenly he

double clicked the key. Instantly it's hands stopped spinning to coincide with those

of his wristwatch at five to three: Its big hand on the eleven, and hour hand almost on

the three.

The lady was in a good mood when she came back, saying, no one had realised she

was late for work, because the hospital had been having a fire drill, so the office staff

had been at their assembly points when she'd arrived.

" Is my bundle of joy ready?" she asked.

"Yes, he's been very quiet, not a sneeze or sniffle from him all afternoon." he

assured her, handing her the rabbit box. The lady thanked the shopkeeper, and left.

Once outside she glanced up at a dark thundercloud, rushed to her car, jumped in

and strapped the box safely into the passenger seat and drove off - but the little white

rabbit inside the box didn't hear the shop bell ring as they left, having snuggled

down contentedly and was fast asleep. Sh!

-:-

EASTER SURPRISE.

" Cock – a – doodle – do! Cock – a – doodle – do!" woke the little white rabbit.

" What's that? It's enough to make a rabbit go deaf," he yawned.

On hearing another sound he was wide awake and went scurrying to hide in the corner of his box. But something grabbed a hold of him! It must be the Cock – a – doodle – do thing, he thought fearfully. Then bravely he opened one eye recognising the lady who had purchased him at the pet shop the day before.

" Did Tom Beddow's cockerel from next door wake you?" she asked. But the little white rabbit was more interested in nibbling the carrot she was holding, gnawing so eagerly that he didn't even notice that she'd put him onto the floor and left the room.

When he had finished munching he began exploring beneath the table, around the chairs and got his head stuck inside the pedal-bin as the lady returned wearing her coat and carrying a length of bright red ribbon.

"What are you doing?" she said, freeing him from the pedal-bin. She tied the red ribbon into a pretty bow around his neck.

"That's more like I,." she smiled, putting him back into the box, sealed the lid securely and carried him to her car. Clunck-click. A seatbelt was strapped around so that he would be safe for a journey. Where is she taking me? he wondered,

Suddenly the car stopped! Through a hole in the box he watched the lady open the window, so took a deep breath of fresh air and listened, hoping to discover where they were going.

"Good morning, I like to have a lie in bed on Sunday morning, but couldn't get back to sleep because your cockerel was crowing Cock – a – doodle do!"

"Ah, It be the hatching season," came a gruff reply. " I had three baby chicks afore I left this morning. Reckon my cockerel be showing off like any proud Dad."

"Does that mean I'll get a lie in tomorrow?"

" I doubt it, there be plenty more chicks hatching as I speak. A hundred years ago my dad's grandpa were a farmer – he'd be far more worried about lamming, milking, ploughing and planting, about now, than he would be about a Cockerel and few chicks... Spring be a busy time, I may live in the city, but us still got green fingers, and the smell of the old farm in us nostrils. I reckon a few early mornings be a small price to pay for **really fresh eggs** Spring, Summer, Autumn and Winter!" he grinned." I be off to work on my allotment now!

" I suppose you're right, Tom 'bye," she called, closing the window, then the car gathered speed leaving her neighbour trailing behind in his van.

After a while they stopped again and the lady got out of the car. The little white rabbit peeped through the hole again as he jogged up and down to the sound of the lady's footsteps until she stopped. He heard a loud knock, knock, and minutes later a little girl's face came into his view.

"Hello Auntie Jane, Come in. I've had lots of Easter eggs!" smiled the little girl .

The little white rabbit watch, as he was carried along the passage to the kitchen.

" I thought you might enjoy a little company, so I've bought you a special Easter gift this year, Sally." said Aunt Jane, handing Sally the large box.

Sally eyes lit up as she thanked her aunt and opened the box excitedly.

" It's a little white rabbit!" she beamed, picking him up, but the little white rabbit wishing to stretch his legs sprang right out of Sally's arms and went hopping about.

" You should call him Snowy with that lovely white fur," remarked Sally's Dad.

" I can't call him Snowy. It's Easter, not Christmas, Dad!"

" Then what will you call him?" asked Mother.

" I'm happy, but can't call him Happy! Happy was one of seven **dwarfs** in that pantomime **Snow White** we saw at New Year," Sally joked, grinning at her Dad.

The man at the pet shop said I'm a **miniature** Dutch rabbit, so why can't I be named Happy like the dwarf ? thought the little white rabbit, as he went hop-pity-hopping as fast as he could around the room and finally sprang onto Sally's lap.

" Hop-pity - hop-pity-hop!" she laughed, stroking him. "I know, I'll call him Hop-pity!"

The little white rabbit thought, it doesn't matter if I'm a big rabbit or a little rabbit, I'm very good at hopping so the name Hop-pity suits me. He winked his approval and jumped down onto the tiles hop-pity – hop-pity hopping around again, before going back to Sally, and straight away they had become the very best of friends.

-:-

HOP-PITY'S HUTCH

Even though you're Sally's pet

Hop-pity; I must regret

You cannot snuggle in my chair

I almost sat on you by there...

-:-

Last night Sally's mother said

She found you underneath the bed!

So father thinking in his head

Went down to his tool shed;

-:-

There found five pieces of plywood

And wire mesh; so that he could

With his hammer, nails and such

Make Hop-pity a rabbit hutch.

-:-

He measured... Cut five lengths of wood;

Planed them, so that they would

Not splinters rabbit's paws.

Then cut one piece in half for doors.

-:-

For sides, in half then cut another,

leaving a back, a base and cover.

In each door he cut a square

Fitting the wire mesh right there.

-:-

He made two rooms with an off-cut

And lock device, so doors would shut.

Hop-pity's home, at last complete

Was the best hutch in Sally's street.

-:-

CRACKING THE CODE.

Above Sally's garden drifted a dark cloud where Father Time, a strange old man had woken up to find a message left on his computer, having forgotten to switch it off before going to bed. He couldn't understand the message, so wrote it down and went to his neighbour to see if she could help.

" Your computer is getting as bad as humans," said Mother Nature " It's picked up a telephone message that must have slipped through the airwaves while someone was putting their clock back, the message must have got into your house somehow."

" I do sleep with my bedroom window open!"

" That explains it. Your computer's left you a text, rather than wake you. Text messages are the latest craze on Earth! " she informed him.

"I don't even know what a text message is." replied Father Time,

" It started when someone invented telegraph. A mathematician like yourself would understand an equals sign: S O S = Save Our Souls. A quick way to request help when humans are in danger."

"The short three letter message would bring help quickly!"

"Yes, that's the idea." She continued, "It was so successful that telegraph was used to send telegrams - which travelled quicker than posting mail in a post-box. But every single letter in a telegram had to be paid for - making it very expensive!"

"Are you saying that humans pay to speak to each other?" he asked.

" Yes, sometimes. Using a telephone is another example; however, a text message can be left on the screen of a mobile phone, -like your computer left this text, for you!

Time and Money rule Earth nowadays, so they use text messaging!"

" If that is true humans may stop talking to each other because it costs to much!"

"No, they abbreviate instead – S. O. S. is an example. Let's look at your text:

"May B late. Park in tickets ran out. I was held up by a traffic warden – have 2 get away, by reversing, Dr. White." Circling **by reversing**, she pointed at letter **B**.

"**May be late,"** she said, and explained that his computer heard the words. "**Park in** could be **Park Inn**. *In* and *inn* sound the same but have different meanings. **By reversing** - Park Inn becomes **inn Park"** she explained, as Father Time interrupted:

" The caller's number was on my P.C. I traced it to East of the River Usk, South Wales, UK. but there is no Park Inn in the area!" he insisted, taking a map from his cloak " There are two parks, named: Woodland; and Beechwood. Beechwood Park stretches from the M4. right down to the A48 – the old road to London.

Mother Nature wrote **May be late in Park.** She explained: **2 = to,** not number *two*! The words sounding alike, but spelt differently - like *in* and *inn*, do too! she laughed.

Father Time grinned, **"I have to get away** - I hate English..! But it can be fun."

" Text messages ruin English! **I was <u>held up by a traffic warden, have to get away</u>.** Mother Nature added, underlined the words, but looked rather worried.

"A traffic warden must be the 21st century's equivalent of a highwayman holding up cars instead of stagecoaches to steal from those who travel in them. - No wonder my computer left this message!" Father Time commented "**Tickets ran out**, Doctor White must want to escape back in time, through the hour's gap, but we don't issue tickets! When humans travel they need to have tickets, don't they?"

Mother Nature agreed. "We'll cross out the word ticket," she said.

"I think the doctor's either worn out from running – or has **run out** from where being held captive - and knows it is too late to slip through the missing hour, so asked, Is it possible to leave later from the park?" Mother Nature concluded.

"May be late in park. I was held up by a traffic warden, have to get away. ran

out. Dr. White, You've decipher the message **by reversing** phrases as we were told.

"We've cracked it!" cheered Father Time. You, a word wizard - and me with mathematics, make a great team. The text was double Dutch, without your help!"

" Well now that we understand the text – What are **you** going to do about it?"

" What am **I** going to do about It! One is born, and moves forward through time! It's straight forward. One simply can't go backward through time!" he retorted.

"Humans turn their clocks back - so why can't you move time back? It's only a matter of time."

" Time is very important!" he informed Mother Nature, yet not wishing or upset her or feel inferior to humans - he agreed, to allow time to stand still for two minutes so that Dr. White might or might not be able to slip back through time - believing such a request to be an impossibility!

" I will do my best to help the doctor," he promised, " but it must be kept top secret. "If humans got to hear about it, they'd all be wanting to return to the past- I'd lose my job because their be on one left on Earth for me to organise time for! "

Mother Nature promised, and told him, that an underground stream flowed from Beechwood's lake to Lliswerry Pond, and agreed to help in anyway that she could.

That's a start, thought Father Time, thanking Mother Nature for her help and the information, before he dashed home to look at Beechwood Park through his spyglass.

-:-

HOP-PITY GOES EXPLORING.

Sally cleaned and put fresh straw into Hop-pity's hutch, gave him clean water, a carrot and some lettuce.

"Hurry up, we are ready to go," called Mother.

" Won't be a minute, Mum," replied Sally, putting Hop-pity back into his hutch.

" I have to go," she told him, closing the doors of his hutch before running off to get into Dad's car. Soon they were speeding along the motorway to the seaside, as Hop-pity munched his breakfast back at his hutch in Sally's garden

When Hop-pity had finished he looked out through the wire mesh window that Sally's dad had fixed into the doors of his hutch.

Where's Sally? Hop-pity thought, impatiently pushing his nose through the wire. Suddenly the door of his hutch swung open.

"Oh!" yelled Hop-pity, losing his balance and toppling onto the lawn, got back to his feet, brushed himself down and checked that he hadn't broken any bones.

"Good, everything seems to be in working order." He sighed, feeling a little dizzy, so decided to sit in the shade beneath the apple tree until Sally returned.

He waited and waited, but got tired of waiting, so hopped down the garden to look for Sally by the front gate. He looked right, left and right again, but there was nobody about. A butterfly came fluttering along and pitched on his nose. Hop-pity twitched his nose and it flew off, so he decided to follow it along the pavement.

It flew around the corner, up the hill and turned again with Hop-pity chasing after it. At the top of the hill Hop-pity squeezed through park railings, following the butterfly, and went bobbing after it across the grass, as the butterfly fluttered between the trees and over a deep ravine where it finally rested on a flower.

"I wish I could fly," whispered Hop-pity, thinking that the butterfly was waiting for him, but Hop-pity couldn't get across the steep ravine where a stream babbled

below. A breeze began to ruffle his fur. He ran to shelter - behind a tree trunk.

"Afraid your journey won't be slow, as reversing now you'll go!" whispered the wind

Waggishly, one's winding up -

Higgledy- piggledy whimsically,

Hop-pity's heart started pounding

To a hurdy-gurdy's melody.

Music grew louder and louder

Whirlwind rushing to its call!

Hop-pity put paws in ears

Rolled himself into a ball.

Then he toppled topsy- turvey

Tumbling down the deep ravine

Hurly-burly helter-skelter

Splashed into the grumbling stream.

Over waterfalls went crashing,

'Neath a bridge; which he found

Led to Beechwood's blarney lake,

To rabbit on; - but almost drown!

-:-

A Tittle-Tattler tried to help,

But standing near the water's brim

The wide eyed Gobbledegook was waiting

To tear Hop-pity limb from limb.

The idle gossip, licked its lips,

Grinning from ear to ear,

Opened its jaws in readiness,

Scoffing, "You rabbit, will disappear!"

It thumped across the babbling lake.

Hop-pity hid, inside the drain

Which systematically swallowed him.

Oh dear, that was a shame!

Gabbling and Gibberish swam

Through the culvert underground,

But clinging onto Hop-pity's ears

Gobbledegook was still around!
-:-

Spinning, swirling, twisting, twirling,

With the monster hanging on

Flotsam and Jetsam both emerged

At a pond near Somerton:

Hop-pity took a big deep breath

Then swung his head so violently

That Gobbledegook let go his ears.

"Free at last!" yelled Hop-pity.

Gobbledegook sank in a pool

Of linguistic lunacy,

The villain now was gone for good!

Butterfly a mere memory.

Our hero swam off to the bank

Clambered up, where daisies grew.

" Thank you, Sire, for saving me,"

Hop-pity prayed, sincere and true.
-:-:-

Hop-pity regained his senses realising that something strange had happened. It was far too quiet - none of the usual horn honking or music blaring from car radios. In fact there were no cars! or houses - except for a few big mansions. Where are all the people? he wondered.

Disturbed by the sound of large animals galloping, he watched them pulling a cart along a road, on top of which a man was seated – but suddenly his view was blocked by smoke puffing from a big black machine containing two men. The machine seemed to be hooked to a chain of huge beads, which puzzled him – until he saw lots of humans inside. They must live in moving homes here, that's why there no traffic, he thought, what is a clever idea,

—

A shadow blocked the sun. Hop-pity shivered and looked up as the long beard of a funny old goat tickled him. It moved its head checking that Hop-pity was alright.

"I was expecting a Dr. White, would have never guessed the **Dr.** stood for **Dutch** rabbit. A **White Dutch** rabbit, that's a bit dirty now." it winked, and wandered away.

Hop-pity was confused, but thought it an animal's paradise to live peacefully in the lovely fields that lay around him. I'd explore the woods at the top of that hill – if I weren't so tired, he sighed. Hop-pity was about to lie down, but became rather worried as a much larger animal with short horns came to investigate.

"**Moo, moo! Who—'s in mm-my mm-meadow**? " it mooed, in a deep voice.

Hop-pity turned tail and hopped off, beneath a gate where he thought he'd be safe.

"Baa, baa," brayed the sheep. There are lots of them! he shuddered, and looking back saw the cow, happily grazing with a few others, none of them interested in chasing him! So he squeezed back beneath the gate and sat contentedly on the grass. One of the cows sniffed and squirted milk over him and they all laughed to discover that Hop-pity was a white rabbit. It was then that Hop-pity remembered he'd been waiting for Sally- but now realised he had no idea where he was or how to get back!

"Oh dear, I'm lost," he sniffed.

It got darker and darker but looking up, the moon's face reminded him of Sally's dad. Perhaps he'll know the way home, he thought.

"Can you tell me the way to Sally's house?" he asked. But the moon couldn't hear or answer him. I really am lost, thought Hop-pity, and began to cry.

—

Sally arrived home and ran down the garden to see Hop-pity, but she found the door of his hutch was open and Hop-pity wasn't inside!

Looking down she picked up the locking peg of the hutch and realised that in her hurry to get off to the seaside she hadn't locked the doors properly, so began searching the garden.

"Hop-pity, Hop-pity, Where are you ? Are you under this hedge?"   she called, searching here there and everywhere - but couldn't find him anywhere.

" Have you seen Hop-pity?" she asked the moon, as it looked down at her. " If you do, take care of him till he comes home" she whispered, before going in for supper.

Sally told her parents that Hop-pity was missing as they ate the fish and chips that her Dad had bought on their way home. She begged to go out looking for Hop-pity again, but Mother thought that Hop-pity had strayed into a neighbour's garden, and promised that she'd go and ask the neighbours if they'd seen him, once Sally was safely tucked up in bed. Sally quickly got ready, picked up her old teddy, and jumped into bed feeling happier as she heard Mother closing the door. Before she switched off her bedroom light.

-:-

HOP-PITY MAKES A MOVE.

Hop-pity the orphan was sad and all alone,

Sitting in a meadow far away from home.

A big rabbit hopping by, said " White rabbit, please don't cry."

" But I am lost." Sobbed Hop-pity, as a tear fell from his eye.

" Come little rabbit, you can stay with my family.

And shortly lots of baby rabbits welcomed Hop-pity.

They played in autumn leaves, but then the winter started

Snow started falling, down their burrow they all darted

-:-

Deep inside their burrow, now all warm and cosy

Hop-pity curled up between Pete' and Rosy.

Mr. Rabbit taught young Hop-pity a lettuce from a swede.

Knowing that when summer came, Hop-pity might leave.

He'd learned to build a burrow. Then he said one day.

"Thank you everyone, but I can no longer stay."

So with Mrs Rabbits parting gift, Whistler her kettle,

Hop-pity left home again, skipping round a stingy nettle.

-:-

Rosy blew a kiss, all the others sadly waved

Thinking that their friend Hop-pity was very very brave.

He hopped towards the wood, with Whistler in his paws

Aware that all wise rabbits live far from farmers doors.

Beneath an oak tree he worked hard, digging out his home…

Where Hop-pity with Whistler no more felt alone

As Whistler babbled on and on, as his water got hot

Telling Hop-pity great stories. So they made tea quite a lot!

-:-

Hop-pity had travelled back to the 19th. century. Sally missed him very much,
but thought she had found a new friend.

SALLY'S SHADOW

In summer, as I walk to school

There's some-one leads the way,

But as our school clock strike twelve

That some-one goes away!

-:-
When the lesson times are over

They follow me back home,

Yet when I'm back in-doors again

Once more I'm all alone!

-:-
Mother said, "It's just your shadow

Lunch-time hiding from sight."

She said, "It is the Sun above

Brings my shadow to life!"

-:-:-

gh together is like a shadow. Silent when side-by-side in <u>most</u> words,

but not in a ghetto of ghastly ghouls and ghosts!
-:-

Can you spot the silent gh word in the poem?
-:-

THE INTRUDER.

It was Saturday, there was no school today so Hop-pity was resting in his burrow when for no reason the bird who lives in his cuckoo clock kept popping in and out.

Coo-coo! Coo-coo! It kept repeating.

" Can't a rabbit get any quiet around here?" Hop-pity moaned, looking up "It's not o'clock or half past!" he sighed, getting out of bed...

" What's that?" he yelled, glaring at a crack that was appearing across his wall.

" I don't know," gulped Whistler, who began coughing and spluttering.

" Are you alright?" called Hop-pity, dashing across to steady his kettle as he held Whistler firmly by his handle.

" That's not working, hang on a minute," he said, as he removed his pals whistling snout and poured some water out of Whistler's tummy.

" That's better," thanked Whistler, taking a deep breath. "I'm not used to water splashing around in my tummy. It kept getting up my snout, Hop-pity!"

" If you're okay, I'll find out what's wrong with our cuckoo clock."

" Good idea," agreed Whistler, "Cuckoo's good company when you're at school."

Hop-pity took the cuckoo clock from the wall, opened the back and fiddled about with its workings. "It's out of balance... I think I've fixed it." he told Whistler.

"You know you should only come out to see us at o'clock or at half past, you silly bird!" he scowled ..."Do you think cuckoo was trying to warn us that there was something wrong?" he asked, waiting for his friend's opinion.

" Cuckoo doesn't say a lot, but you could be right," Whistler answered.

" I'll take a look outside that crack could have been caused by an earthquake!"

" We don't have earthquakes in our country!" Whistler informed him.

Hop-pity almost dropped the cuckoo clock as earth and stones fell into his kitchen.

A hole appeared in the wall through which a dark eyed hairy face peered in at him.

" Who are you?" he whimpered, with Whistler trying to hide, thinking the intruder was about to gobble them up for its lunch...

" Oops! Didn't realise I was near your burrow, Hop-pity" came a friendly voice.

" You scared us, Mrs. Mole. Better come in now that you're here. I don't think you can do much more damage. Why didn't you use the entrance?" asked Hop-pity.

Mrs. Mole sat down. "It's a long story," she began,

" Farmer Beddows has sold a lot of sheep, so with Shep the sheepdog they've moved the rest up onto the hillside. Now Farmer Beddows is planting potatoes in our field. He was ploughing when my husband got caught up in the machine. Mr. Mole is badly injured," she sighed. "In the future Farmer Beddows will be ploughing and planting every Spring and digging up his potatoes to sell at the market right through Summer and Autumn. The sheep were really good neighbours, we loved living beneath that field, but it's not safe to live there any more.

"Ellen and Marigold offered to look after Mr. Mole in their pigsty – it's not the cleanest of places for someone so ill, but having no choice I was so glad of their help. The Trotters are so kind but have enough to do looking after the piglets. Not wishing to inconvenience them too long, I was rushing to build a new home - when I accidentally dug through your kitchen wall. I'm very sorry," she apologised.

" Don't get upset. I'm worried that Shep might loose his job having less sheep to look after. He always warns me when Farmer Beddows is about! " frowned Hop-pity.

" Don't worry. There's enough sheep left to keep Shep busy!" replied Mrs. Mole.

" That's good," remarked Hop-pity. "I'm sure with Dr. Squirrel's help your husband will soon be well again. I'll help you dig a new burrow ready for his return."

" That would be a great help, Hop-pity." replied Mrs Mole who was much happier.

" Dr. Squirrel lives in the oak tree above, I'll get him to call at the pigsty about any medication Mr. Mole might need. While I'm out could you pop Whistler on to boil? There should be enough water left in him for us to have a nice cup of tea."

"Certainly Hop-pity, I'm glad I dropped in now." she smiled, putting the kettle on.

Whistler was sad about Mr. Mole, but his tummy was soon warm and bubbling, pleased that the intruder was only Mrs. Mole who would soon be living next door.

Hop-pity had fixed his cuckoo clock. It was now something o'clock, but what o'clock? Try to find out the answer as the cuckoo bird chirps the right time:

"Coo-coo! Coo-coo! Coo-coo! Coo-coo! Coo-coo!

Coo-coo! Coo-coo! Coo-coo! Coo-coo! Coo-coo!"

-:-

CLEVER CLOGS.

Considering herself to be a working animal, earning her keep like Shep the Sheepdog. Copy the Cat didn't think she needed to go to school. Her master, Farmer Beddows didn't like every animal – he didn't like Foxy who sometimes broke into the hen house.

But he loves me, because I kill the mice that eats his corn that he sells to be ground into flour so that the baker can make bread, she thought, lazing in the sunshine, watching the windmill blades turning in a light breeze.

She thought of herself as Queen of the barn and windmill, knowing that when in residence the mice and bats kept out of her way. Hanging up-side-down from the rafters the bats even bowed as best they could when she visited. – or so she believed!

—

Copy began to yawn. This will never do when I'm on duty, she thought, afraid that watching the windmill blades turning might send her to sleep. So she decided to walk up the footpath between the Maindee Hall and Maindee Park mansions, to visit Dr. Squirrel or Hop-pity, as she had plenty of time before returning for elevenses.

Mrs. Beddows, her excellent cook, would have finished the milking and scooped off the cream ready, by eleven o'clock, she purred, licking her lips.

"Hygiene, deportment and *precise* manners merely *predict perfection* for a *pretty* pussy as *precious* as *me*," she mewed, smoothed her fur coat with her tongue and went to check her appearance in the lake. She pouted, blinked at her reflection and adjusted her tail so that it curled slightly at the end and raised it on high.

Copy strutted across the tramway and up the hill toward a small select woodland area beyond the gentlemen's residences, where she expected to wander in the shade with her orphaned friend Hop-pity – who'd fallen on hard times - having once been a pet living in the garden of a family who had been devoted to him. But Copy had a

wasted journey having forgotten most of the wildlife would be at Mr. Owl's School.
However she heard a bird trilling merrily and saw a bird perched in a tree.

"That bird has a beautiful voice - the best I've ever heard !" she muttered jealously.
" But what's the point of practising to achieve such a voice, when one can have others
sing for you" she consoled herself, but determined to prove her superiority, eyed the
trees.

"I can climb – better than any bird," she purred smugly, recalling Mrs. Beddows'
words: That her cat was a relative to the king of the jungle! Copy ran to the tallest
tree, stretched up, sharpened her claws on its bark and began to climb - to prove that
like lions, cats might not hit the high notes - but could certainly climb the tallest trees!

Skylark sang sweetly as it hovered high above. Copy hadn't noticed Skylark- but
it had seen Copy and was pleased to see her climbing the tree, so sang beautifully
aware that the cat was not after her eggs! Skylark stopped singing and checked to
be sure she wouldn't give away her nests location, before diving down into the grass.

Crow had also been listening to Skylark's sweet song. All was still quiet, except
for Copy purring above the sound of rustling leaves, which convinced Crow that she
must be climbing up to his nest! Spreading his wings he rapidly flew across to
land on a branch above Copy, between her and his nest – to protect his chicks.

Copy snobbishly stuck her nose in the air as she reached the top of the tree's trunk.
Finding it divided into separate branches, she paused to decide which route to take.

Crow watched cautiously, fearing for his chicks as Copy turned onto the branch!

" You may be able to sing, but I'll reach the top of this tree first," boasted Copy,
as she walk majestically towards Crow. As she did, he expanded his chest as if he
were ready for a fight – yet hopped further away from Copy, tempting her away from

where his chicks were curled up asleep in his nest.

Copy assumed that by hopping away, Crow must be scared. He would make a tasty meal, she thought, edging towards him. Crow retreated further, keeping just out of Copy's reach, tempting her to follow... She did, slyly threatening him...

" You'll be sorry – I've only taken the trouble to climb this tree to congratulate you on having such a wonderful voice."

Crow chuckled, realising that Copy thought the skylark's singing, had been his!

" If that is true, why climb this tree instead of this one I was singing in? If you had, you could have heard my lovely voice more clearly! " he cawed.

" There's no reason for you to speak so gruffly, after my good intentions... It's alright for you, your claws curl around the branch," she hissed, gingerly tightroping along the branch, as Crow moved further back again.

" I've only got two legs, you have four! You'll be alright," cawed Crow.

That must be true, thought Copy. Mrs. Beddows says that two heads are better than One. Yet having four legs didn't seem to be helping. In fact, Copy was having trouble to keep her balance. As the branch narrowed it was jerking with her every move - and having four legs made it impossible to turn on the narrow branch. Copy realised she couldn't get down, not that she planned to - her mind on having Crow for lunch.

Having reached the end of the branch, Crow cawed with laughter. Copy was angry - eager for revenge - took a final step, her big green eyes glaring. She transferred her weight onto her back legs. Steadied herself, lunged and pounced at Crow, who flew away, happy knowing that his chicks were safe – but Copy tumbled and went howling, whining, screeching, squealing, until she landed on the grass with a bump.

–

Ginger Tom - the cat Farmer Beddows referred to as That Moggy - had followed Copy, so raced across to help her.

"You are very brave Copy. Are you alright?" he asked.

" My feelings are bruised but thankfully we cats do have nine lives," she sniffed.

" True," agreed Ginger, who wiped her tears and helped her to her feet.

"You climbed right up this hill and right up that tree! you must be exhausted. I'll walk home with you – just to be sure you're alright."

Feeling dazed, Copy nodded, her tail dragging the ground as she limped home.

" Bye, I'll see you tomorrow, to make sure you're okay," called Ginger, as Copy squeezed through the cat flap, happy to be home, to the comforting smell of fish cooking and her elevenses waiting - even if it was twenty-five minutes to two!

-:-

CAT-KIN OR LAMB'S TAIL.

It was a bright Spring morning as Hop-pity went leaping across the fields to the farmhouse. He crept below the hedge bordering the garden. Copy the black and and white cat darted over thinking Hop-pity was a mouse to share between her kittens.

" It's strange to see you here. Where are you going?" asked Copy the farm cat.

" You're right. I don't come near the farmhouse in case Farmer Beddows is about," replied Hop-pity, " but Mr. and Mrs Mole were wondering how the sheep have settled in now that they're living on the hillside."

" I saw Mr. Mole at the pigsty after the accident. How's he getting on now?"

" He's recovering, but hasn't ventured out doors yet... Sh,.. he might see me! " whispered Hop-pity, referring to Farmer Beddows who was coming out of the farmhouse. Copy turned and seeing him ran over and began running between the farmer's legs.

" Get out of the way. You'll have me over in a minute!" shouted the Farmer, as Copy the cat continued to be a nuisance until Farmer Beddows was out of the gate.

" You clever cat!" said Hop-pity, thanking her for drawing the farmer's attention away from where **he** was hiding.

Copy decided she'd enjoy a walk before meeting Ginger, so when Farmer Beddows was out of sight, they set off to the hillside together. They'd reached the bottom of the hill when Hop-pity, suddenly stopped looking up at a hazel tree.

" Look at all those caterpillars hanging from the branches," frowned Hop-pity.

" I've never seen so many before."

" Caterpillar!" laughed Copy. " They're not **cat**erpillars. They're **cat**kins," she added proudly.

" They're not like cats – not you, Ginger or your kittens!" remarked Hop-pity...

" They're lamb's tails!" interrupted Sheep, looking down on them with an air of superiority.

" They do look more like lamb's tails than any cat I saw at the pet shop," agreed Hop-pity.

" Some people call them lamb's tails, others call them catkins!" scowled Copy.

" Pussy willows are in bloom at this time of year, too!" she said and purred smugly

The sheep didn't argue knowing that Copy was right! But wished he hadn't bothered to walk down to meet the visitors, so turned to rejoin the flock.

" Please don't go," called Hop-pity. "I've come especially to find out how you've settled in, because Mr. and Mrs. Mole were concerned about you having to move."

The sheep stopped and turned its head indignantly.

" The Moles were **good company**,.. kept very much to themselves and **never upset anyone!**" replied Sheep, glancing at Copy.

" Good of them to enquire. We're happy enough, the grass is much better here. Tell them the ewes are lambing at the moment. By the way, how is Mr Mole?"

" He's doing fine. Dr. Cyril Squirrel lives near, so calls to see him most days."

" Good! Glad he's going on alright. I'd better be off, my wife's expecting twins and she'll never forgive me if I miss the birth! Thank you for calling," Sheep replied before wandering back up the hillside.

—

" Foolish creatures, I don't know why Shep the sheepdog bothers with them." said Copy, who after checking the windmill suggested they walk back to the hay barn together, where she'd planned to meet Ginger Tom and their kittens for lunch.

" Mrs. Beddows calls those flowers Catkins. She fills a vase in Springtime and puts it on the kitchen table to remind her that the cold Winter weather is over."

" They don't look like flowers!" frowned Hop-pity, as they passed beneath the tree.

" Oh, they are," Copy assured him." But they're not highly perfumed or have brightly coloured petals to attract bees. They're self-pollinating, you know" and Copy went on to explain all about self-pollination as Hop-pity listened, until they reached the hay barn.

" I enjoyed our walk. Now it's time I checked what the mice are up to. Farmer Beddows gets very angry when the mice mess up the hay or steal his corn from the mill, you understand. See you again!" Hop-pity waved as Copy crept silently into the hay barn.

—

As Hop-pity got near home he saw Mr. Mole's head poking up from the ground.

" Good news, what..! Dr. Squirrel said, it's time I got out and about." he grinned.

" Morning. Nice to see you're well again," replied Hop-pity. "Tell Mrs. Mole that the sheep are happy and send their love. I'm glad I went to see them because I've learnt something very interesting."

" Now if you'll excuse me, I'm off to enjoy a nice cup of tea with Whistler. I want to tell him all about catkins…or lamb's tails! " Hop-pity smiled.

" Silly animals. bickering about the flowers being named after cats or sheep because they resembled their tails… Life's too short for all that – Mr. Mole's lucky to be alive," he thought, as he scampered along, and down into his burrow to find his best friend patiently waiting.

-:-

In the 21st century Sally was still missing Hop-pity so went to look for him.
Do you think she will find him?

SALLY'S SEARCH.

Rain has stopped! Shining through

The rainbow's coming into view.

Soon the colours fade away

So Sally went out right away

Brisk and early like a lark

Through the streets, to Beechwood Park,

She crossed the road to the other side

Where the park gates were open wide.
-:-
"Here's Tom Beddow in his van,

He tries to splash me if he can.

He's going to sell his eggs and veg.

But leaves a pool with coloured edge

'Cause petrol's leaking from his van.

He's being chased by a policeman

Waving his arms to make him stop

With Mrs Jones from the wool shop!"

The puffing pair stop with a gasp.

"Have you seen Hop-pity?" she asked

" Sorry Sally." both replied

The policeman made a note with pride.

" We'll tell you if we find your pet

I'll make enquiries. Glad we met."

Then Sally went into the park

Searching 'round till it was dark
-:-

"Where are you, Hop-pity?" she called

As down beneath a hedge she crawled.

Her clothes were getting really mucky

But alas, she wasn't lucky

Falling down on muddy path

Said, "Now I'll have to take a bath!"

Yet bathing in the rainbow bubbles

Sally soon forgot her troubles.

-:-

"What's that strange noise?" enquired Harry Hedgehog.

"What noise?" questioned Hop-pity, raising **his** floppy ears. "Oh, that noise! It's probably Owl trying out his latest invention. Shall **we** go and see what he's up to?"

"Rather," replied Harry Hedgehog.

Hop-pity dashed ahead as Harry tried to keep up with **him**, until Hop-pity slipped and fell over getting tangled up in a greasy old newspaper.

" Look at that mess!" **he** moaned.

"Are you alright Hop-pity?"

"Yes," gulped Hop-pity, But my fur's all sticky. "It's all very well inventing things, but I wish Owl would clear his mess up. I could have broken my leg!"

"It's not like Owl to leave litter around. He was the one that made the Litter Tidying Law - telling **us** that litter causes disease and could start a fire!" puffed Harry, catching up with his pal.

The couple stopped and stared across at the most untidy human **they**'d ever seen sitting with his eyes closed, leaning against the trunk of Owl's tree.

"It's a man," whispered Harry.

"I can see it's a man! Harry. But what's he saying?"

"He's not saying anything, he's snoring!" Harry Hedgehog informed Hop-pity. "My wife snores all winter, but if **she** snored like **him**, I wouldn't get any sleep!"

"He's awfully scruffy," murmured Hop-pity. Who'd crept closer to investigate.

"Be careful, Hop-pity. He might be a friend of Farmer Beddows."

"Farmer Beddows wouldn't go anywhere near him the way he stinks!" said Hop-pity, holding his nose. "The fellow needs a bath! I don't think he's ever washed. His tatty clothes need washing and having the seams stitched up. They're falling apart!

He doesn't seem to care about his appearance a bit. Look he's got a bottle of water with him. I feel like pouring it all over him - to give him a wash, Harry."

" Don't do that, Hop-pity, you'll wake him."

" It's not water anyway," came Owl's response, from a branch overhead.

" You're up early," said Harry, glancing up.

" Couldn't sleep with the bellowing noise that man's making!" replied Owl.

" He should get off home, have a bath and tidy himself up. We don't want his litter or the likes of **him** lying around here; do we?" added Hop-pity.

" Doubt he's got a home!" said Owl.

" What do you mean, every ones got a home! When I lived in Sally's garden I had a hutch, and she lived in a lovely cottage."

One by one other woodland animals gathered around listening to the conversation.

" Well he should build himself a home like we do!" said Hop-pity, turning to the others for support as he continued. "Humans are stronger and supposed to be cleverer than us! There's no excuse he simply hasn't got a leg to stand on.

Owl smiled, knowing that the man had had too much to drink, fallen down, and was sleeping off the effect of the alcohol. The evidence was clear from the word Beer printed on the bottle that was lying beside him.

" Admitted the man has behaved very badly, but will any of you speak in his defence? He's certainly in no condition to speak for himself," added Owl.

There wasn't a murmur from the captivated audience. Harry sat thinking - which was most unusual for Harry. Someone should speak for the man, he thought.

" I'll... I will!" He suddenly shouted, to everyone's amazement.

 Owl disappeared for a moment, reappeared, threw a horseshoe down onto the grass and hammered three times on a branch. " Let court commence." he squawked.

33.

" We've heard Hop-pity's opinion of this man's conduct so who agrees with his view?"

The group nodded approvingly, much to Hop-pity's pleasure.

" Good, that will save us a lot of time! Harry will now defend the accused. Do you wish to call any witnesses?" asked Owl.

" I haven't got any witnesses to call…"

" Call me!" buzzed Buzzer the bee.

" Order. Silence in court!" Owl hammered. "Do you wish to call this witness, Harry?"

" I suppose so," replied Harry.

" In that case you may take the stand," said Owl, nodding at the bee.

" Where shall I take it?" joked the bee as it flew across, wiped its foot on its jumper, placed his foot on the horseshoe and took the customary Oath of Truth.

" I promise: To help my mate-zz, close all gate-zz!

Never uproot a plant, fell tree-zz

Or spread disease-zz - by leaving litter!

Report the zz-sight of flame or flicker.

I zz-swear on oath: my words be true!

Claiming luck from law-zz horse zz- shoe."

"I need z -some luck! 'cause there's-z no flowers about. Z-so I can't do my job," he added.

"There's a lot of buttercups growing down by the stream!" shouted Hop-pity.

"Thanks, Hop-pity. I didn't expect the horseshoe to work so quickly. Can I go now?"

" Certainly not!" shrieked Owl flapping his wings angrily. " This court is in motion and I demand silence!"

-:-

A NARROW ESCAPE.

"Order! Order! Now before we continue I wish to remind you that we are dealing with a very serious matter."

Order was restored. Everyone sat silently as Owl turned and nodded toward Harry.

"You may question the witness."

" I don't know what to ask my witness," said Harry. Everyone giggled, knowing that Harry often fell asleep during lessons at school. They all thought Harry was as silly as a sheep, being very stupid to have volunteered in the first place.

Not wishing to look foolish, he asked. "Do you know this man? And secondly, did you see him throwing litter about?

"Zz-sorry, and Zz-sorry! I'zz not zz-saw him before, and did not z-see anything!" came Buzzer's reply. Everyone thought the bee was as silly as Harry

"Then why are you wasting our time!" demanded Owl.

"I'zz not! I just knows-zz he's-zz a drone. And drone's-zz is-z las-zy things-zz! I agree it's a serious matter, 'cause me and my mates-zz stings-zz drones-zz to death!"

Everyone looked at the bees sharp sting, and shuddered.

"I understand your reasoning, but you may stand down, Buzzer." Owl remarked, turning back to Harry. " Do you wish to call any further witnesses?"

Harry looked very worried, frowned at Mr. Owl and shook his head rigorously, feeling extremely dismayed and ashamed that the witness he had just called wanted to sting the man to death, when he was supposed to be defending his client.

"As there are no further witnesses, Harry, you may commence your summing up."

Harry looked puzzled. Summing up? We do that at school, he recalled, so began:

" One's two is two. Two two's make four. Three Two's…"

"Not that kind of summing up!" interrupted Owl. Just get on with defending your client," he sighed.

"I'm sorry, Mr. Owl." replied Harry, who thought for a moment. Then rose to his feet, cleared his throat, took a deep breath and hoped that what he was about to say didn't add to his embarrassment.

" We have no witness who actually saw the man littering our woods. I'm not really sure whether it is our wood anyway," he added. "We just live here!"

" He wouldn't know our Litter Tidy Law! So I ask you" he continued, turning to everyone. " If he doesn't know the law, how can he be responsible for breaking it?"

"Good point, Harry! We must put some signs up," demanded Owl.

Harry was elated by Owl's comments and gaining confidence continued:

" The man maybe unaware that he could have set the woods alight, putting our homes and lives at risk. Maybe his home burnt down so has nowhere to live! Without water he couldn't wash himself or his clothes." Harry smiled, feeling rather pleased with himself. He was about to continue. When Cyril Squirrel, shouted,

"Then he should use the stream and build a new home, like we do!"

Owl, glared at the culprit "You've got nothing to shout about. Squirrels just find a hollow tree to live in!" and squinting one of his big dark eyes, hammered angrily on the tree branch and demand that nobody was allowed to speak without his permission after Cyril Squirrel's rude interruption.

" Silence in court!" Please continue your case for the defence," he added, thinking that his pupil Harry Hedgehog was doing rather well, considering it was Harry!

" The man may look well enough but I don't think he is. He's been sick over there. Look at that dreadful mess on the grass." he pointed... "Humans aren't like us, they need money to buy bricks to build their houses... This poor man doesn't seem to have any, so how could he afford a house. We're lucky, we don't need money to buy bricks to build our houses. We should…"

The man suddenly stretched, gave a yawn and frowned at the animals. Catching sight of Hop-pity he sprang to his feet.

"I can see a little rabbit, roasting over an open fire when I catch you!" he grinned, revealing gaps between his large discoloured teeth and charged towards the terrified crowd. Everyone scattered. Hop-pity gasped, almost passing out from the man's foul smelling breath, as he lurched toward him, but Hop-pity managed to slip out of his grasp, turned tail and ran for his life - the man racing after him.

Hop-pity's heart missed a beat on seeing Farmer Beddows ahead of him. Hop-pity watched him raising his shotgun to shoulder level - his eye to the sight and finger on the trigger. As the farmer came racing towards him, Hop-pity knew that being trapped between them he had no chance of escape on this occasion. Looking around he was wondering which way to go, and saw the man running off down the path… Even he's scared of Farmer Beddows, thought Hop-pity, leaping sideways, to crouched down beneath a prickly blackberry bush hoping its thorns may give him some protection.

"Get off my land, stealing milk and messing my farm up - and take the rest of your kind with you!" yelled the farmer, "You'd better make it snappy, 'cause if I catch any of you, you won't be round to tell the tale!" he bawled.

Hop-pity's heart was pounding, if only he were nearer one of the entrances to his burrow, he thought. Fortunately Farmer Beddows didn't spot his hiding place, but went charging passed, followed by Shep the Sheepdog -who slackened his pace -

"Don't worry he's more interested in that fellow than he is in you!" barked Shep, before resuming speed and went racing down the path after his master.

That was a narrow escape, thought Hop-pity, best get home – I can't wait to see Whistler's friendly face - I could do with a rest and a nice cup of tea!

-:-

HOP-PITY.

A mischievous little rabbit

Goes hopping through the lane,

He makes some country folk annoyed

I suppose I should explain.

-:-

People welcome calves and chicks,

Spring lambs and ducklings **too**,

We all live very happily

'til Hop-pity comes hopping through.

-:-

He nibbles at the lettuces

Then runs across the meadow,

Or pulls the tasty carrots up

Till chased by Farmer Beddows.

-:-

Mrs. Jones works at the wool shop,

She likes soft rabbit fur

And thinks, mischievous Hop-pity

Would make a nice jumper!

-:-

Spinning wool from fleece of sheep

That live on Tom Beddows farm.

I think the **two** of them

Plan Hop-pity much harm.

-:-

I heard her tell the farmer,

She was good at cookery

Saying she'd make him rabbit pie

If he'd like to come to tea.
-:-

Now the farmer has a shot gun

Which he carries on his round

Searching for ears amid his crops.

So Hop-pity flops his ears down,
-:-

He hides between the cabbages

Till it's safe **to** cross the dell.

I know exactly where he lives,

But I'd never, never tell.

-:-:-

Farmer Beddows shears his sheep in Spring and sells their fleece to make

wool.

JENNIE THE DONKEY.

Hop-pity scampered from his burrow to find the woodland rustling with lea**ves**.

" What are you doing?" he laughed, seeing Harry rolling about in them.

" Enjoying myself! It's Autumn, almost time to hibernate. Come and play – it's great fun."

Hop-pity jumped up trying to catch the lea**ves** that were falling from the tree**s**.

" Catch one for me, Hop-pity. If you catch one before it hits the ground it'll be a lucky **leaf**. My legs aren't long enough, so I can't jump up to catch leaves like you."

" Got it!" cried Hop-pity. "It's a red one, will that do?"

" Red's my favourite colour!" chuckled Harry. "With its luck I might sleep right through Winter. If I wake I can't get back to sleep, it's too cold in Wintertime!"

" You do look funny, your prickles are covered with leaves!" laughed Hop-pity.

" Are they? If my prickles are good at leaf collecting we could clean up the whole wood, Hop-pity! I'll stab them up and you can take the leaves off me to make a big pile ," said Harry Hedgehog curling up into a ball and rolling about again.

" Don't do that!" squawked Owl who'd been watching from above. "Leaves rot, the worms eat them and the waste produce feeds the trees for next years growth! – Oh, watch out, the pair of you," he urged, " hurry up, there's something coming!"

 They both dashed for cover as a lot of **caravans** began to rumble passed. Harry and Hop-pity recognised the scruffy man who was driving the last **caravan.**

" What's up with you now?" yelled the man at his sad donkey, and began thrashing it with his whip.

"Get on there, Jennie… Hurry, the others are way ahead!" he yelled, hitting the donkey again and again. It stumbled but somehow limped along trying to catch up, as the man raised his whip shouting "Get a move on, you lazy good for nothing thing."

The caravan ahead stopped, a boy jumped out and ran back to assist him.

"What's up, Jennie having trouble again? I'll get the spare horse from the horse box and hitch him up instead, or you'll never get there, Uncle Ed," said the boy.

The scruffy man agreed and jumped down from his caravan.

Harry and Hop-pity watched them remove the harness and fit it onto a big horse.

" Come on, Uncle Ed. We'll leave Jennie here, she's not worth wasting a bullet on! Nobody will know it was us who left her once we're on our way." The boy called as they clambered back into their separate caravans. There followed a tugging on their reins and the horses were off at a gallop, leaving poor Jennie huddled on the ground.

When the caravans were out of sight Harry and Hip-pity crept from their hiding place to see if they could help the donkey.

" Keep her completely still!" squawked Owl flying off to get Dr. Cyril Squirrel.

Harry and Hop-pity obeyed, till Cyril Squirrel came scampering along with his first aid bag. He sent Hop-pity to the brook for clean water, while he examined the leg. It was sprained, not broken, so he bandaged it – and had fastened the bandage with a double knot when Hop-pity returned. Then Cyril Squirrel pointed out Jennie's injured foot, caused from hobbling around on a broken shoe. He removed the two metal sections and bathed Jennie's wound in the clean cool water.

" That's better, at least the cut isn't septic." he reassured her. Then sprang up to land gently on her back and began to sponge where the whip had lashed her

" This cold water will bring out any bruising and help the swelling go down. You'll be feeling much better in a day or two." he nodded confidently.

" Can I do anything else to help?" asked Hop-pity.

" Yes. Jennie will need feeding up. Donkeys like carrots just like you, Hop-pity. I prescribe plenty of carrots - the carotene may improve her sight too! And with the proper care she'll soon be up and about. When her foot heals, she'll need to be fitted with a new horseshoe – you'll find a pile that has been discarded by the blacksmith in a much better condition that those Jennie has been hobbling about on, poor dear…

Sorry I can't stay, must dash. I have to finish collecting for my hibernation or I won't be around to look after you all next year, you understand. You wouldn't want me to starve myself, would you?" he joked, winking at Jennie, hoping that she would have put on a little weight by the time he saw her the following Springtime.

" I'm leaving you in charge of the patient, Hop-pity. Wake me if necessary." Dr. Squirrel instructed, before running off to finish collecting enough acorns for Winter.

-:-

Hop-pity made a good friend in Jennie the donkey – especially discovering that She had watched the scruffy man's wife making sweets and toffee apples!

By Spring Jennie was well, so she opened a <u>sweet</u> shop in the wildlife village that lies deep in the wood and made friend with Rosy who worked in the cake shop next door.

-:-

Between you and me: Shep the sheepdog tells Jenny when Farmer Beddows will be at the market. Then she visits the horse and ponies that live on his farm.

-:-

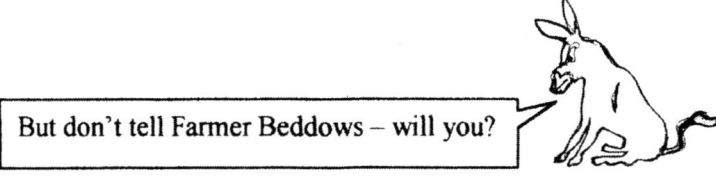

But don't tell Farmer Beddows – will you?

<u>HAPPY ENDINGS.</u> (Plurals)

Simply **add s.** For **endings: <u>sh</u>, <u>ch</u>, <u>x</u>** and <u>s</u> – add <u>es</u>.

Mainly **f becomes v** - and **- y becomes i**, then add <u>es</u> .

It's as simple as pie.

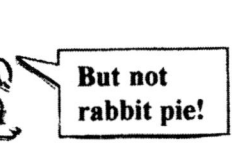

But not rabbit pie!

Simply <u>**add s when a vowel proceeds y**</u>. That's all for now, here's the farmer! Bye, bye.

-:-

THE POT OF GOLD.

Spring was in the air, the geese flying to Russia, after over wintering on the lake.

Mrs Swan wished them safe journeys before returning to her nest a little worried.

" See you next year," quacked the local ducks

" There they go... Here they come!" cried Hop-pity.

" What are you on about?" yawned Cyril Squirrel looking down from his tree, still

rubbing the sleep from his eyes

" The geese are leaving, but here come the swallows and swifts from Europe. I'm

amazed you're awake to see them!" exclaimed Hop-pity

" We'd better welcome them," yawned Cyril, making his way to the ground.

" Hello, you're usually asleep when we arrive, Cyril," chirruped a swift

" The early bird catches the worm," joked Hop-pity.

" Not necessarily," replied the swift, "If I stamp about the worms think it's raining,

so come to the surface of the ground for a drink – Swift by name, swift by nature!

Designed for speed – and I have a very swift beak when worms surface!" it chuckled.

" Had a good trip?" asked Cyril

" Tiring, but I'm a bit peckish after the flight. At lease there were no casualties,"

came the eager eyed swift's reply, as it pounded about anticipating a juicy lunch.

"You'd better watch out, Hop-pity" chirped a swallow, informing him that a goose

he'd met on his journey had mentioned posters in America offering big cash rewards

for: **Billy the Kid dead or alive**! - probably because the cowboys like boots made of

the kid's soft leather. The American ladies liked it for shoes too, but also wanted his

special fur to make angora wool for knitting."

Mrs. Swan nodded sadly in agreement.

" Billy the goat's skin is special – just like angora wool is in Britain," she sighed.

43

" But what has that got to do with me?" asked Hop-pity.

" Angora wool is made from rabbit fur, too!" warned his friend Cyril, " I believe that woman from the village wool shop wants your beautiful white fur, Hop-pity. She's only friendly with Farmer Beddows because he shears his sheep for her to make wool – and you must admit Farmer Beddows is very keen on catching you, isn't he?"

" Shearing sheep is okay! Sheep get too hot in summer, and their fleece grows back by wintertime; but he's not shearing me!" yelled Hop-pity, running off to hide.

Cyril wanted an excuse to stay talking, hoping to hear more news. Noticing a rainbow in the sky, he pointed,

" Isn't that a lovely rainbow?"

" Not as good as the ones on the ground in Holland!" chirped one of the birds.

" Rainbows are not on the ground!" laughed Cyril.

" **They are in Holland**!" agreed the birds, nodding their beaks at Cyril.

Hop-pity's from Holland, he'll know if the birds were telling the truth, thought Cyril, so ran off to catch up with Hop-pity.

" The birds said, rainbows are on the ground in Holland, Hop-pity. Is that true?"

" How would I know?" answered Hop-pity.

" You're a Dutch rabbit and Dutch rabbits come from Holland, don't they?"

" Yes," agreed Hop-pity, "but I was a tiny bunny when I came across on the ferry."

" Fairies don't exist!" laughed Cyril. "You told me you came with a butterfly."

" I got lost when I followed a butterfly, then swam through a tunnel and arrived in Lliswerry pond at Somerton Farm. Anyway I'm more worried about being a wanted rabbit Dead or Alive like Billy the Kid." he shuddered... "I'd be safer in Holland... They say there's a pot of gold at the end of a rainbow – and if rainbows are on the ground there, we could find that pot of gold!"

" That makes good sense to me Come on, let's go!" cried Cyril.

" Not in so much of a hurry, Cyril! We could stowaway on a ship bound for Holland," suggested Hop-pity, " but we'd have to watch out for ship rats on board!"

"You mean treacherous sailors, like the rat who was whipping Jennie the Donkey."

" No! Ship rats are very big black rats with long tails, big eyes and ears!" Cyril shuddered. "Don't want to scare you, but they have horrible fleas," warned Hop-pity.

Sally told me that hundreds of humans died from being bitten by ship rat fleas, so the children sang and played A Ring of Roses. – I'm glad you'll be with me!"

"Why?" frowned Cyril, " I'm not sure I want to come now."

"Because you are a doctor! But I've no idea why they sang Ring of Roses."

" A Ring of Roses sounds like a wreath to me!" scowled Cyril Squirrel.

" Don't' worry, she taught me the song, I'll teach it to you," Hop-pity assured him,

"Let's make plans then," he shrugged, thinking: Gold, enough to build a hospital!

Hop-pity wondered how he could wake Dr. Cyril Squirrel, knowing that doctors who worked the night shift often slept till lunchtime. He had the idea of digging up carrots for the journey, tying one of them onto a piece of string and tying the other end of the string to Cyril's foot before he went up to bed. When Hop-pity woke early - as he always did, he could pull the carrot and the string would pull Cyril's foot to wake him up too!

With their plans agreed, they decided to leave for Holland the next morning – Cyril suggesting on board a clean looking ship – so having put their plan into action They practised singing Ring, a Ring of Roses, and when Cyril Squirrel was word perfect he scampered up the oak tree to his home and threw the carrot end of the string down to Hop-pity.

" That's fine, the string's long enough. I can reach it. See you in the morning!"

" Yes, Okay I feel a bit happier now. 'Night Hop-pity."

—

Jennie the Donkey couldn't sleep that night so went wandering through the wood, and seeing the carrot dangling from doctor Cyril's tree he took it in his teeth and ran off pulling Cyril out of bed. Cyril came tumbling down from his tree and went hopping after Jennie on one leg.

" Stop! Stop!" shouted Cyril.

" What's going on down there?" squawked Owl.

" Had to be up early to get to Holland. We're going to find the pot of gold that lies at the rainbow's end," Cyril explained.

" Dutch rainbows are not that kind of rainbow. They're stripes of bright flowers that look like giant rainbows on the ground as we fly overhead," chirped a swallow.

" It's only Dutch flower growers that get a pot of gold by selling their flowers all over the world!" laughed Owl.

" There's no point in you going to Holland then, is there, Cyril?" shrugged Hop-pity."

" Nay. Ne-ver mind," neighed Jennie the Donkey.

" Please don't go alone Hop-pity – a ship rat might get you ! whinged Cyril.

" You have friends here. We'll all keep a look out and warn you if the farmer's about," added wide eyed Mr. Owl

" You seem pretty fit, Jennie. Well enough to have given me a few bruises!" joked Dr. Cyril Squirrel, who was pleased that his patient had made a full recovery... Hop-pity agreed to stay with his pals knowing that they could be trusted and everyone was happy once more.

-:-

RHYME AND REASON..

In the 21st century Aunt Jane had called around to take Sally out.

" Where are we going? " asked Sally.

" Do be patient, Sally and fasten you seat belt, you'll soon find out! " smiled Aunt Jane as she released the hand brake.

" You were so happy when I gave you your pet Hop-pity at Easter – but he's been gone so long I doubt he'll be coming back," she said, pulling up outside the pet shop.

"I thought I'd buy you another. Come on, you can choose whichever one you like," said her aunt, reaching for her handbag.

" I don't want another rabbit!" replied Sally scornfully.

" Can't I persuade you to change your mind? Perhaps you'd like a kitten instead!"

" No," frowned Sally " I only want Hop-pity!"

" Well, if your mind's made up there's nothing much I can do about it... I know, we could buy some cakes and have a picnic in my garden – How about that?"

Sally agreed, so they bought the cakes and it wasn't long before Sally and her aunt sat enjoying their picnic in the sunshine.

" What would you like to do now?" asked her aunt.

" I don't know. I usually go out looking for Hop-pity. – but haven't had any luck." she sighed. " It's nice just being here in your garden for a change – can I just stay here a little while longer, before you drive me home?"

" Of course you can. I like this garden too. I made up a poem about you and me sitting here – I'll go and get it," she said, putting the crockery onto the tray.

Sally was surprised to learn that Aunt Jane wrote poems -she always seemed much too busy to be doing that sort of thing.

When Aunt Jane returned, she said that writing poetry in her garden helped her to relax and took her mind off worrying about things she could do nothing about.

" Like when I'm sad worrying about Hop-pity, you mean? "

"Yes," her aunt nodded and began to read:

Bluebells dozing in the dell

Roses climb my wishing well

Shadowing where the fairies dance…

Then goblins charge with sharp grass lance.

–

" What are goblins?" asked Sally looking around the garden.

Aunt Jane explained that her neighbour had a gnome fishing at his pond - and that goblins were like gnomes but instead of being friendly they were mischievous little imps causing all kinds of trouble.

"I call these - flowers with faces" she smiled, pointing at some pansies. Then by pressing the sides of an antirrhinum flower on each syllable, it seemed the flower was reading as she continued:

Pansies watch with faces round,

Antirrhinum stand - speech bound

As daffodils blow out reveille

Waking the lily of the valley!

–

Aunt Jane explained that daffodils were Spring flowers, so she'd cheated because the centres of daffodils looked like trumpets. Sally grinned and her aunt continued:

Violets hide beneath the hedge

Waking hedgehog from his bed

" What's wrong?" he yawned - half awake,

" I guess a look I'd better take."

–

The ant army marched on its way

Singing, It's up to us to save the day.

A plan of action they agreed

With black and yellow suited bees.

—

"Infantry advance, to garden gnome –

Then onward to the fairies home..!"

The airforce z-zoom- z out of their hives –

Had goblins running for their lives.

—

The ants and bees made them retreat

With cuts and stings – attack complete!

Once more my garden's back at peace…

A foolish story - for my niece.

—

Sally didn't think her aunt's poem was foolish but pleased that her aunt had written it especially for her - and realised, that while she had been listening to it she forget her own problem.

When Sally arrived home she played in her own garden until it began to rain. She went indoors, Later she tried writing a poem herself – making lots of mistakes, until her Mum helped with the rhyming – and when Dad came in from work Sally told him that she had a surprise for him – and read:

I'm snapping off some daisy heads

Imagining they are fried eggs

My crispy bacon falls from trees

Completing breakfast, if you please!

—

I often play with my tea-set

But it's not fun without my pet.

I watched the ants, a buzzing bee,

A ladybird crawled on my knee.

—

" Fly home now! I'm telling you -

Your home's on fire!" I blew - It flew -

Hop-pity please come home too!

Now I'm sad. What shall I do?

—

I think I'll give his hutch a scrub,

So with soapy water I started to rub

Bubbles sparkling like rainbows bright

Makes me think Hop-pity's alright…

—

I hope that he'd be back one day

Then I'll know he is okay.

His hutch is dry. I laid fresh straw

Making a carpet on his floor.

—

If he comes back from where he's been

His hutch is waiting nice and clean.

Then I'll be pleased -- that's for sure!

And we'll be happy evermore.

—

Hop-pity would be proud of you, Sally – I certainly am," praised her Dad…

Sally started to wonder where Hop-pity could be –

Nobody knows, except you and me, that Hop-pity's back in the nineteenth century,

In love with Rosy, living happily. But what happens next? We must wait and see!

-:-

HOP-PITY IN LOVE.

"Your tea's gone cold again today. What's wrong with you lately?" asked Whistler.

" Nothing's wrong," sighed Hop-pity. "I'm fitter than the cow who jumped over the moon!"

" You couldn't hop over a teeny wh – eeny, wh-ite wind flower today. Wh – y won't you tell me wh –at is wrong?"

" It is something I need to sort out for myself," snapped Hop-pity, who rushed off along his burrow and went down to the lake where it was quiet.

Whistler is my best friend but he's not a rabbit – he's not even an animal. He couldn't possibly understand how it feels to be in love, thought Hop-pity.

" Something troubling you, Hip-pity?" asked Mrs. Swan who had glided across the lake to see him.

Thinking that she might be able to help, Hop-pity explained that he loved Rosy Brown rabbit but thought it would upset Whistler his kettle – who was his very best friend.

" Then don't tell Whistler until you find out whether Rosy loves you. If she doesn't there will be no need to tell your friend Whistler anything, will there?"

" That's true," agreed Hop-pity "but how can I find out if Rosy loves me too?"

" No problem. It's Valentine's Day soon. So you can make a card explaining how you feel about her. She comes to the lake for a wash everyday."

" I know she does," smiled Hop-pity. The problem is I'm too shy to speak to Rosy and don't think I've got the courage to give her a card telling her I love her."

" I understand," replied Mrs Swan thoughtfully… " A couple of children came here on a tandem last week."

" What is a tandem?" asked Hop-pity.

"A bicycle with more than one saddle – so both the children rode here on it together – but that's beside the point! Please stop interrupting, Hop-pity. To continue, I was watching them carefully because the boy lit a fire at the water's edge."

" He could have set the countryside alight - Sorry, Mrs Swan. Do go on…"

" They were having a picnic and he was cooking sausages in a pan on the fire. – He thought it best to cook where there was plenty of water near in case things went wrong, I guess… Anyway they were good children, made sure the fire was out and thought they'd taken all their litter home – but one of their pop bottles rolled under that bush over there," she pointed out, lifting her wing. " So make her a Valentine card but don't write who it's from – just leave a clue that it might be from you. Then roll the card up and put it into the lemonade bottle like a cork. I'll be looking out for your return. Then roll the bottle down the bank to me."

Hop-pity looked very puzzled and began shaking his head.

"But the Valentine card isn't for you!" he argued,- but Mrs. Swan laughed loudly.

"Bottles full of air will float, so I can be your postman by paddling the bottle across to Rosy when she comes to wash on Valentine's Day. I will know by her response whether she likes you too," she nodded. "If she does then you can tell Whistler – explaining it is good to have two special friends and that you'd like to invite Rosy for tea. Tea and pancakes would be good, as it will soon be Pancake Day. Whistler will enjoy watching you tossing pancakes and that will put him in a good mood for when Rosy arrives.

"That is a good idea. Thank you for your help, Mrs Swan," he said, hopping off to see if Owl would give him some paper to make a Valentine card… Hop-pity worked hard on his card. He included one clue in the verse and another at the very end instead of writing who it was from, as Mrs. Swan advised. So his Valentine card read:

Will you be my Valentine

Not for a day or two

But for as long as I'm alive

To love and care for you?

I love you – ROSY

From X X X - X X X X.

Early next morning Hop-pity went to the lake and gave the card to Mrs. Swan.
Mrs. Swan delivered the Valentine card to Rosy when she came to have her wash.

Rosy soon worked out that Hop-pity wasn't sure how long he would live, knowing
there might be a reward for his capture – because his fur would make lovely soft
angora wool just like Billy the goat's fur.

She wondered what future Hop-pity might have, but was pleased to discover that
he wanted to spend it with her. Rosy blushed and twitched her nose with happiness as
she counted the kisses – one for each letter in the name Hop-pity!

Mrs. Swan watched Rosy's joyful expression as she'd read her Valentine card.

" Well I never – I wonder who sent you that!"

"I think I know" smiled Rosy, "but I'll be late for work if I don't hurry," she
grinned, springing to her paws, then blew Mrs. Swan a kiss and went hopping and
skipping up the hill and through the wood arriving at nine o'clock – just in time to
open the cake shop.

-:-

HOP-PITY'S BIRTHDAY.

Rat-a-tat woke Hop-pity. He sprang out of bed and hopped to his entrance. Pigeon the post had been – and was flying off again.

Obviously no time for a chat this morning, thought Hop-pity picking up the mail. He began opening his letters – when something fell from one envelope dropped into his burrow and rolled along the hallway.

"A shiny two pound coin!" he yelled scampering along to catch it, then read his card:

"Been too busy with the sheep to get anything for your birthday. Lucky I actually remembered! Love from Shep."

Hop-pity set off to buy some honey and on arriving, he knocked on the beehive ready to dodge Buzzer the big bumble-bee as he came buz-zzzzing out, wearing his black and yellow jumper.

"Can I buy some honey?" asked Hop-pity.

"Zzz-orry, Zzz-old out," buzzed the bee. Can't you Zz-ee I'm buzz-y?"

Hop-pity looked at Buzzer's aggressive sting, and went leaping away thinking he would buy some sugar lumps instead.

At Jennie the donkey's sweet shop, Hop-pity struggled stretching up to reach and turn the doorknob but managed to open it and hopped inside.

"Please have you any sugar lumps?" he asked.

"Na-y, na-y. N-ot toda-y" replied Jennie the Donkey.

"Never mind, maybe I'll buy a nice cake from the bakers next door," he said, looking into the window, but he didn't fancy any of the cakes on display and was about to leave, when Rosy the pretty rabbit who worked there came out.

"Hello, how are you?" she asked, twiddling her floppy ear with her paw. Hop-pity was surprised to see her and stuttered

"It's my b-birthday today. I'm not quite sure how old I am, but wanted to buy a cake to celebrate."

"Sorry not on Wednesdays," she grinned, Hop-pity winked, before heading down to the dairy at Somerton Farm, where he found Bluebell, Buttercup and Snowdrop.

"Have you a tub of cream or even a yoghurt? " he pleaded.

"No-o yoghurt. M-ore to-mo-rr-ow." mooed Bluebell, and looking up together

"Mil-king n-ow," they mooed very loudly as a warning.

Hop-pity's heard footsteps and trembled on seeing Farmer Beddows standing in the doorway of the milking shed and realised why the cows were mooing so loudly. The farmer didn't have his gun, but by blocking the exit Hop-pity could not escape!

" I'll get you this time!" shouted the farmer as he dashed after Hop-pity, but Hop-pity dodged around and between the cows' legs. Hearing a clatter he turned to see that a bucket of milk had tipped onto its side spilling, leaving a trail of milk as it rolled along followed by Farmer Beddows sliding along the floor on his bottom!

"Now look what you've done, you good for nothing rabbit!" he bawled.

Needless to say, Hop-pity didn't hang around to hear the rest of his conversation, but charged back towards the wood, where he saw his friends waiting near his burrow.

"Here he comes!" flapped Owl, who had a pot of honey for him.

"I found this under my hedge, catch! It's for you," called Harry Hedgehog, rolling a golf ball in Hop-pity's direction. Copy the farm cat purred trying to give Hop-pity a tub of cream, as Cyril Squirrel threw a bag of sugar lumps from his oak tree - just missing a little green fog who came springing along to see what all the commotion was about.

"Haven't got time for all that, Farmer Beddows is after me," Hop-pity panted, racing down into his burrow.

"You look as though you could do with a nice cup of tea," welcomed Whistler.

"No thanks, the farmer's been after me. I'd rather cold water, " he puffed.

Rosy who had arrived with a large box, said that she'd seen Farmer Beddows covered head to toe in milk and had been looking very angry as he went into the farmhouse.

"No wonder Hop-pity's hiding." They all laughed.

"It's safe to come up, Hop-pity. The farmer gone home to change," hooted Owl.

Hop-pity's face peered through his entrance. "Are you sure?" he asked timidly.

"Yes, it's safe. And I've made something special for your birthday," smiled Rosy. Guess what Rosy had made..? A big birthday carrot cake. Do rabbits like carrots?

—

Mrs Brown had always said, the way to a rabbit's heart was through his stomach. When Hop-pity tasted Rosy cooking they started to go on picnics together, Hop-pity was leaving Whistler alone more often but he didn't mind. He was very pleased to see Rosy and hear news about the Brown Rabbit family. He recalled the day that Mrs Brown Rabbit had found him rusting away under the hedge. She'd picked him up gently in her mouth, the rain water tickling his tummy as it splashed about inside him as she'd hopped along. He smiled to himself remembering how excited her family had been and how welcome he was made, when she'd arrived home with him. So seeing Rosy and Hop-pity together made Whistler very happy indeed.

-:-

Can you remember all six of Hop-pity's birthday presents?

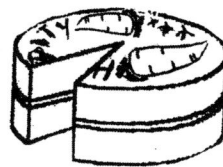

MAYBE MAY DAY.

One morning Rosy was over at Hop-pity's making lemon-mint tea with the water Whistler had boiled. Hop-pity gave Rosy a daisy chain and bunch of buttercups, then knelt down and asked Rosy to marry him. Rosy said, "I may or may not."

" Well make up your mind," frowned Hop-pity.

" I'd marry you tomorrow but Big Brown Rabbit – my father, would have to agree. He may or may not allow me to marry you, Hop-pity."

"You stay here and have your tea with Whistler or it will get cold, while I go and find out," he cried, turning sharply as he sped off along his burrow.

Rosy began giggling. Whistler started whistling with laughter - but began to splutter, splashing water through his nostrils - here, there and everywhere – making a terrible mess all over Hop-pity's new worktop.

"Are you alright?" Rosy asked, finding a cloth to wipe up the mess before Hop-pity got back.

" Yes, hup…hup…hup..!"

" Now you've got hiccups," she said, patting his back until he recovered.

" I've never seen Hop-pity so excited. He must love you, Rosy."

Rosy lowered her head shyly, bit her lip and wondered what her father would say.

" I'm surprised that Hop-pity was brave enough to ask me – I've hoped he would for ages. I need a cup of lemon mint," she said, pouring boiling water into a cup, adding a sprig of clean mint and squeeze of lemon. She left it to brew for a moment, removed the mint, added a little sugar and stirred. Then picking up the cup Rosy sat down and began to sip it.

" That's better. Now all We can do is wait till he comes back."

They waited for a long, long time till Hop-pity returned, puffing and blowing.

" Wh- what did he say?" asked Whistler excitedly.

Hop-pity couldn't answer. He flopped down on a cushion and panted trying to get his breath, then shook his head.

" Your Dad said, he may or may not agree – then asked me about my prospects. I told him I have a very nice home where we can live. Told him that I loved you and would take good care of you, Rosy, – but he said, that there was a price on my head so I may not be around to look after you. He is right, I know that is true."

" Are you saying he won't let me marry you?"

" Well maybe, maybe not."

" What do you mean – Maybe?" interrupted Whistler.

" Maybe – it depends."

" Depends on what?"

" Whether you may or may not want to get married if we may not be together long."

" Of course I want to marry you!" she shouted, "it's better we share the time we have, enjoying every second of every minute. Every day of every week – maybe we will have months or even years. You are so clever Hop-pity. Who knows, Farmer Beddows may never catch you!"

" Wh –wish I come to your wh-wedding," sighed Whistler.

" You're coming – we'll want a good cup of tea to go with our wedding cake… He will be able to come, won't he, Rosy? "

" Of course he will. I'll ask Big Brown Rabbit to give him an invitation."

" I'll carry you to the orchard myself, – in fact, I was wondering if you'd be my Best Man. You'll have to whistle extra loud to make sure I'm up early that day."

" I can't be your best man, I'm your best kettle –your only kettle - but Wh- what day must I wake you early?"

" Our wedding day, of course," grinned Rosy " - it may be May Day!" she said,

and they all burst into laughter.

-:-

A DAY TO REMEMBER

Back at Big Brown Rabbit's burrow, Rosy's Mum was thinking about her only daughter's wedding. She knew Rosy would marry Hop-pity and wanted the day to be extra special, so planned what she'd do, hoping everything would work out fine.

On the Wedding Day Whistler saw a spark from the fire set one of the maypole ribbons alight. He was afraid to blow his whistler off to speak, in case the hot water for the guests tea, scalded one of them. So he whistled loudly and kept on whistling - but no one took any notice. They thought he was just enjoying all the excitement of the wedding, until Mr. Mole realised that Whistler had been trying to warn everyone about the danger they were in.

Hop-pity said, that Whistler had done a very good job. Mr. Mole said, he was the best in the world.

Whistler was confused – the best what in the world?

" Am I the best kettle?" he asked hopefully " I wouldn't want to be the Best Man or the best animal!"

" You were the one that gave the warning, so that we were able to keep the fire in check until the firemen arrived. The woods and our homes didn't get burnt down and no one was hurt. The wedding could have been a disaster without you." said Big Brown Rabbit. " Three cheers for Whistler. The Best…"
Everyone cheered. Even the farm animals could be heard mooing, grunting and braying in the distance - as Hop-pity turned to his bride and whispered:

" He really is Best kettle in the whole world!"
Whistler had the most wonderful day in his life but had had enough excitement. so was content to get home safely. He thought his memories would last for ever as he gazed at the picture hanging on the wall of the burrow,

Mrs. Brown Rabbit had gone to a lot of trouble to make the day a great success

and it was the most wonderful day anyone could remember. So her dream came true.

A DAY TO REMEMBER.

My daughter's getting married.

She's such a lovely doe,

I'd like to make a wedding dress

But how? I just don't know.

I'll go and ask the silk worms

And with Spider's help

Perhaps we'll make a wedding dress,

I can't do it by myself.

Silk worms agreed to help,

Then Spider supervised

And with silk the silk worms spun

Spiders left their webs – to weave from nine till five.
-:-

Mother picked a strong pine needle,

In it she made a hole,

Cut out and stitched the wedding dress –

As Mr. Mole made the Maypole...

Copy let the secret out, which

Hop-pity confirmed through Otter

So bought the ring. Himself a suit

Manufactured by B. Potter!

By haggling he'd purchased both

For the Birthday coin he'd had.

They were married on the May Day

Mother wept of course – but not 'cause she was sad:
-:-

Rosy looked so beautiful

Holding her bouquet,

Friends dancing 'round the Maypole

Cheering – "Hip, hip hooray!"

Mice were flouncing their frills

Dressed prettily, in pink –

A very special beetle

Dyed the silk, I think!

Birds twittered as the blossom fell

On Rosy's veil and dress.

Smart Hop-pity did Rosy proud!

Tears of joy - words can't express.
-:-

Mole's maypole went up in flames –

He dashed for water from the well.

Fire engines rushed along the road

Each vehicle rang its bell...

The fire put out; one fireman saw -

Rosy in her dress – and said:

"I must have smoke still in my eyes"

Then frowned and scratched his head.

The couple. paw in paw, went off

To feed the Swans and Ducks –

Who loving the taste of wedding cake,

Quacked thanks and wished them: Good Luck!

-:-:-

FRIEND AND NEIGHBOUR.

It had been snowing for three days. Hop-pity woke and shivered.

"Good morning Rosy," he said, filling Whistler with water for a nice hot cup of tea. Soon Whistler was bubbling a merry tune, then began whistling loudly to let Hop-pity know the water was boiling. Rosy got up and made the tea to go with their breakfast.

Hop-pity finished breakfast and hop-it-y-hopped along his burrow and looked out.

" It 's stopped snowing," he called, "I feel like going out to stretch my legs."

Rosy ran along the burrow with Hop-pity's welly-boots, told him to take care and gave him a kiss.

Harry Hedgehog and Cyril Squirrel will still be asleep, he thought, as he looked up at the branches hung with icicles that dripped little holes in the snow.

" Morning Hop-pity," chirped Robin as he flew overhead, landing some distance away. I could go and play with Robin, he thought, so put on his scarf, socks and pulled on his four welly-boots. He felt snug and warm, as he went leaping across to where Robin was wrestling with a big juicy worm.

" Got you!" chirped Robin as he pulled it right out of ground.

" Can you come and play?" asked Hop-pity.

" No, It's taken me ten minutes to get breakfast this morning," Robin said, looking at the tasty meal wriggling at his feet. "Have you met our new neighbour?" he chirped. Hop-pity frowned and shook his head.

" He's staying down in the meadow. Must go now, Hop-pity, it's too cold for hanging about in this weather, even in my new red jumper." He shuddered, and picking up his worm Robin took to the air, waving his wing to Hop-pity, his breakfast held firmly in his beak. Hop-pity decided he'd go and meet this new neighbour, so trudged through the snow to the meadow.

"Hello, I'm Hop-pity." he said, looking up at the stranger's cheerful face.

" Pleased to met you. Won't shake hands, it's a bit difficult with you wearing your four welly-boots," smiled the stranger.

"Do you plan on staying around here?" asked Hop-pity.

"Oh yes, it's a lovely place and everybody's so friendly. I plan to spend the rest of my life living here. It's the finest place I've ever visited."

"Have you come far then?" enquired Hop-pity.

"Oh yes, I'm quite a traveller, ' been all over the world."

"How interesting," said Hop-pity, but wasn't sure whether to believe the stranger.

" To have travelled all over the world, you must be very old," said Hop-pity politely.

"It doesn't take that long travelling by air. As for my age, never really thought about it. I guess you're right, Hop-pity. I must be rather old," the stranger replied.

Suddenly Hop-pity caught sight of Mr. Beddows coming across the meadow.

"Watch out, he's got his gun!" Hop-pity warned his friend. I must be off, I'll visit you again," he promised, as Farmer Beddows raised his shotgun to take aim. Hop-pity's fur was white like the snow, so the farmer couldn't see him as he ran off.

That was a narrow escape, thought Hop-pity, puffing and panting as he reached his burrow. Then he slipped off his welly-boots and went into the kitchen.

"The farmer almost got me that time," sniffed Hop-pity rubbing his paws together.

"Are you alright?" worried Rosy. Hop-pity nodded.

"Glad you're safe," whistled Whistler.

Hop-pity   told them about their new neighbour, but as he put his paws on his kettle to warm them, Whistler shouted –

"Your paws are freezing, Hop-pity!"

65.

"Sorry. It's cold out. Luckily my wife makes the best tea in the world," he hinted.

Rosy had made carrot stew, so she put Whistler on to boil, and suggested they had an early night because Hop-pity said it hadn't snowed all day. If the weather really was getting better Rosy wanted to be up early to get the washing done.

"That's w-wonderful. I'm glad the wh-weather is getting better, I hate being cold," whistled Whistler, who was feeling the water warming in his tummy.

After they had finished their tea, Rosy cleaned up, Hop-pity wound cuckoo clock up. They wished Whistler a goodnight and were soon snugly tucked up in bed.

On Monday it was sunny, so Hop-pity helped with the washing and hung it out to dry for Rosy, on Tuesday Rosy managed to get the ironing done as Hop-pity cleaned the burrow. It wasn't till Wednesday that he was able to visit his new friend again.

-:-

THE MEADOW MYSTERY.

Hop-pity set off along the path through the woods to the meadow, looking for his new friend. He searched but couldn't find him anywhere. He asked Robin, and Shep the sheepdog who'd just finished work, but they hadn't seen him either.

"We need to form a search party!" suggested Hop-pity, who explained that he was worried because Farmer Beddows had been aiming his shotgun at them both, when they were last talking together. "I warned him, but couldn't stay, thinking that Farmer Beddows was going to shoot me!" Hop-pity explained.

" I'll wake the others up," said Robin. "It'll be quicker for me to fly back to the wood. Be back ASAP." He chirped, leaving Shep and Hop-pity to go on searching.

Harry Hedgehog didn't want to get out of bed, but as soon as he heard what had happened he was on his way. On hearing the news Dr. Squirrel sprang out of bed in case there'd been an accident, arriving with his medical bag and a magnifying glass!

"I examined a mound of white stuff on my way here," Dr. Squirrel informed them.

So it was decided that they should all go and have a look at the white stuff.

"It's only snow," chirped Robin, as Harry Hedgehog joined the search party.

"What is snow?" Harry and Cyril asked together.

"We always have snow when you're both fast asleep," Hop-pity explained looking down at the mound of snow. "However, I think this is the spot where I was last talking to our new neighbour," he informed the others.

"P-perhaps Farmer Beddows didn't l-like him, so shot and b-buried him under the s-snow," sneezed Harry, shivering with cold.

" Wouldn't think so, he's always nice to me," interrupted Shep the sheepdog.

" Nice to you. You must be j-joking!" beamed Harry. "Pats you on the head and tells you you're a good dog. D-don't you realise he only feeds you because you d-do his job of looking after his s-sheep? You're no more than his slave. If you didn't work so hard, he wouldn't care w-what happened to you."

Shep leaned his head to one side thoughtfully, then began to sniff around the pile of snow, while Cyril began inspecting the area with his magnifying glass for clues.

"What are you doing?" chirped Robin.

"Looking for evidence," replied Cyril Squirrel

"What do you hope to find?" yawned Harry.

"The bullet, from Farmer Beddows shotgun, of course! "

"There's nobody under the snow," grinned Shep, " I knew he wouldn't hurt anyone"

Hop-pity doubted Shep's remark, but asked "Well, does anyone have any ideas?"

"How about Foxy? I know he took a turkey just before Christmas and I haven't seen him around lately! He could be in hiding," barked Shep the sheepdog. Foxy could be responsible for their friend's disappearance, they all thought, till Cyril pointed out that in his opinion, Foxy only took the turkey to feed her cubs, because they would have died without food! And if Foxy hadn't taken the turkey, Farmer Beddows would have killed it for Christmas anyway.

Shep stood quietly remembering that before Christmas his master was out to kill Foxy for running off with the turkey. Yet he had killed many turkeys himself! Shep began to wonder if Farmer Beddows was as wonderful as he'd always thought.

Shep's thoughts were disturbed by Owl squawking

"What are you all doing down there..? You should be in bed hibernating, Harry!"

" I know," yawned Harry.

"I should be asleep too," Cyril commented, "but our new neighbour's disappeared. We think he may have been murdered!" said Cyril, shaking the snow off his tail.

"Murdered!" remarked Owl, "What makes you think that he's been murdered?"

"Only three days ago, he told me that he planned to spend the rest of his life living near us, down in the meadow at Somerton Farm. But he's vanished!"

"This is a very serious matter!" squawked Owl, "I'll get the bird-force on the case. I'll tell them to keep their heads down and eyes open. They can make enquiries and report any sighting back to me and also the whereabouts of strangers in the area.

Owl paused, taking out his notebook and rubbed his claw on an evergreen plant.

"I need to take details: Description and information of when and where the new neighbour was last seen."

Shep, Hop-pity and Robin agreed that they'd last seen him three days earlier, wearing a scarf, blue bobble hat and was.. Owl stopped writing, looked up and asked.

" Was he white in colour, and cold to touch?" The three nodded.

"Yes that's him, have you seen him?" asked Hop-pity excitedly.

"Yes," replied Owl. He was the snowman built by Farmer Beddows' children! But with the sunshine we've had the last few days he's melted away."

The group of friends looked very puzzled.

"So where is he now?" asked Hop-pity.

"The sun has taken him back up to form clouds. He's off on another journey around the world. I suppose he did live with us all his life on this occasion. Sometime in the future he'll come back to Earth, like pieces of a jigsaw puzzle, landing in another country where children will put him back together again. Now the mystery has been solved, I think it's time you all went back home and got some sleep."

They were all happy that the snowman had visited them on his journeys. Dr. Cryil Squirrel gave Harry medicine for his cold, and told Hop-pity he would be calling to see Rosy on Tuesdays. Hop-pity looked rather puzzled…

"Is Rosy ill?" he asked.

"No, but I'm glad you helped her with the washing yesterday – It is not for me to say, she'll tell you when she's ready."

It was getting dark so they all went home, got into their bed and everyone fell fast asleep - except for Hop-pity who lay awake wondering if Rosy was ill. Dr. Squirrel said that she would tell him when she was ready, but Hop-pity could not rest. he was more worried about Rosy than he was of Farmer Beddows' gun. So Hop-pity turned his thoughts to clouds floating around the world drifting in the blue sky, which made him feel very tired, until at last he yawned, turned over and fell asleep.

-:-

CUMULUS NIMBUS.

" Hello, Hop-pity."

" Hello to you too," replied Hop-pity wondering who was speaking to him, till he looked up

" Oh, how did you get here, Mr. Snowman? I thought you were off on your travels."

" Well I am but thought I had been very rude to leave without saying Good bye after you had been so friendly towards me," smiled the Snowman.

" Most thoughtful of you to drop in. Could I make you a cup of tea or something?" asked Hop-pity.

Oh no, please don't go to any trouble on my account. I'm not stopping, just thought I'd call as I was passing. I have to get back on my way, " he said, holding out his hand in a friendly gesture. Hop-pity took hold of the Snowman's hand -

" Gosh, you are cold."

" One has to be, otherwise you'd have a pool of water in your home," he grinned. You could come with me – you might enjoy the experience. I've seen where you live so thought you might like to see where I spend most of my time. - It's up to you of course. At least I will have made the offer."

There was no way Hop-pity was going to miss such an opportunity, so he quickly put on his welly boots and the Snowman took his paw, saying, There is just one thing you must remember.

" Oh yes, and what's that?"

" We are going to Cumulus Nimbus where it is most important that you do not mention anything hot, because those who live there believe that just speaking of heat will make their cloud combust because many others that look like it have done. "

"Yes, alright I'll remember, " agreed Hop-pity excitedly, but what does combust mean?" he asked, finding he'd left his burrow and was drifting upwards.

" I thought everyone knew – combust means explode!"

Hop-pity's eyes span like Catherine wheels as he realised they were going to a land that might explode - but it was too late to change his mind, they were already on their way. So without a word more he listened as the Snowman rambled on.

" I rarely go to Cumulus Nimbus, but Jack Frost says the weather has been strange lately. Planet Earth is getting hotter – even the ice at the Poles is melting, so the oceans are rising, causing floods. Jack wants my opinion regarding whether the snowmen would mind if he organised more snow storms to try and cool Earth down.

" I haven't been asked to attend such an important meeting for hundreds of years – so I must be there on time! I shouldn't think he'd mind if I took you along. We are very good friends, – and as we don't often get visitors from Earth he might arrange a guided tour for you while we talk - it shouldn't take long. When we're through we can be off to my place before I drop you home again , okay?"

Jack Frost comes to Earth in Wintertime, thought Hop-pity, having heard Cyril Squirrel say that Jack Frost had been doing a bit of decorating, and remembered the white paint in the woodland being wet when he'd touched it. Jack had completed the job in one night, so there must have been a full moon he guessed, as it looked very pretty but didn't last long - Now I might actually meet him, he thought.

Hop-pity looked back till the familiar woodland where he lived faded from view. They flew on gliding over pine trees and a high mountain, that the Snowman called Snowdon, before escalating even higher into the sky like a couple of kites.

Hop-pity felt the crisp fresh air in his nostrils the higher they went. He was feeling the cold biting through his fur, yet Up... Up... Up... they went, until the Snowman pointed out a very big dark cloud, which reminded Hop-pity of the anvil he'd seen at the blacksmiths shop where he and Owl had taken Jennie the Donkey to have her new horseshoe fitted when Dr. Squirrel had asked him to take care of her.

" Prepare for landing!" commanded the Snowman, as they gently glided down towards the foreboding cloud.

" Careful now, land on your back leg first and then use your front paws as a brake to stop you rolling over – We don't want to go bumping into anyone, do we! "

Hop-pity shook his head and made a successful landing.

" Well done, that was an excellent touch down, Hop-pity. Now follow me." Hop-pity followed in the Snowman's tracks.

" It's a good job you told me to put my welly-boots on," said Hop-pity who was struggling to keep up – while reading the street signs - Snowflake Walk, Sleigh Ride Avenue, which was long and much busier. They turned into Icicle Square, where the Snowman turned to Hop-pity and told him that all the important people lived in that part of town - pointing out Mother Nature's cottage and Father Time's manor house which had a large clock tower – its clock numbering one to twelve with the names of the months painted on its outer circle.

Hop-pity gazed up at it, as the Snowman explained that Father Time was a funny elderly gentleman with a long beard which sometimes tripped him up because he was always in a rush and rarely looked where he was going - his mind wondering when he might have a little relaxation. He liked cutting Mother Nature's lawn with his scythe - a welcome change from his lifetime job of cutting off the days, months and years.

" No, he's not there" sighed the Snowman, looking over Mother Nature's hedge. "Didn't think he would be - Ah, there he is busy, juggling numbers at his office," he laughed, pointing up at a window in a nearby building.

" He's a good juggler, isn't he?" laughed Hop-pity, looking up as they passed.

They began to climb steps leading to a beautiful building which the Snowman informed him had been designed by Jack Frost. It twinkled and sparkled all the colours of the rainbow.

Hop-pity rubbed his paws and tried burying them in his fur to keep warm. When they got to the top step, there was a shrill sound of trumpets and of the portcullis grinding upward with a jingling from the motion of the two diamond threaded ropes that glistened in the light.

They passed beneath into a courtyard, through a beautifully carved door - where Hop-pity found himself in a long passageway where they were stopped and the Snowman questioned.

"You'd best stay here, Hop-pity." Snowman continued on his way, leaving him with two odd looking characters he assumed to be castle guards.

Hop-pity felt rather uncomfortable as they looked him up and down and whispered together. He looked along the corridor but there were no seats to sit down and as it was no warmer inside the building than out, Hop-pity decided to watch what was going on outside from the doorway. But he was stopped in his track -

" Where do you think you're going? "

" You were asked to remain here!" interrupted the accompanying guard, before Hop-pity was able to answer the first.

" Look, he's up to something!" said one.

" What are you doing that for?" questioned the other, glaring at Hop-pity.

" I'm only rubbing my paws together," whimpered Hop-pity wishing the Snowman would come back.

"Why are you rubbing your paws together?"

" Because I'm very, very cold." He pleaded, " Is there somewhere I could warm my paws?"

" I told you he was up to no good – friction causes heat and you know what that means. Watch him - he'll be after a M-A-T-C-H next!"

" I'm not a f-f- footballer," whimpered Hop-pity, having worked out what the letters spelt.

" If you've something to say, then speak up." So, raising his voice, Hop-pity said,

" I'm **f-freezing**. Do you have a radiator or **f-f- fire -** I could warm by? If not I'll **f-f-freeze** to death. I'd be alright if only I could get w…" Hop-pity was interrupted.

"Did you here that? He should have never been allowed landing rights!" the guard yelled, posing to attack, as his partner pulled a rope that set alarms ringing.

Hundreds of guards appeared armed with sharp icicles like swords - Hop-pity suddenly remembered he'd broken the promise by mentioning the forbidden word.

Without hesitation he turned and ran. The two guards set chase, others with their sharp icy swords joining them in earnest pursuit.

" After him, and show no mercy or we'll all be doomed," ordered their commander – as Hop-pity made it through the doorway across the caught yard – but they were gaining on him. He just managed to squeeze beneath the portcullis as its jagged edge was descending. He went rolling down the steps and scrambled back onto his paws only to be faced by a crowd of townsfolk who immediately chased after him. Hop-pity ran as fast as he could, looking this way and that, searching for an escape route – the sound of the portcullis rising again -

"Snowman, Snowman!" he cried, glancing back over his shoulder not daring to stop, but his cries seemed to be in vain. The angry crowd was almost upon him as he stumbled, losing his welly-boot. Not daring to stop he raced on – his back leg like a block of ice as he panted out of the grey walled town, its glittering building lost in the mist – but they were still in pursuit. He could hear them. Up a grey hillside he charged, loud rumblings and streaks of light flashing as he looked back.- in his haste toppling right over the edge of Cumulus Nimbus. At first floating, then Down… Down… Down into a cold dark abyss. A loud rumbling filled his ears – a great dragon appeared, roaring as it breathed bright orange streaks of flashing fire. Hoppity continued to fall until he landed heavily on his shoulder with a loud bump!

He'd obviously hurt himself – but at least he had escaped the army of Cumulus Nimbus. They would have surely killed him, he thought - clenching his shoulder. He'd survived and his enemies would never attempt that dive to destruction.

Rubbing his arm to ease the pain, he squinted through the darkness as a familiar voice filled the air - It wasn't the Snowman's – this was a sharp chirping voice - a friendly voice, a bird's voice…

"What on earth are you doing down there?" Cuckoo asked, waking Rosy. "Cuckoo, Cuckoo, cuckoo."

" Three o'clock - and what **are** you doing down there, Hop-pity?" frowned Rosy.

" I've just fallen off cloud – can't remember its name. I went there with my friend the Snowman, it was great till…" Hop-pity suddenly stopped and looked around…

" Trips with snowmen? You've certainly had your head in the clouds - Cloud Cuckoo Land, no doubt, " laughed Rosy.

" You must be right. I'm glad to be back. My dream turned into a nightmare."

" Probably brought on by the storm. Gosh, you're freezing, good job you built our burrow under the oak on the hill. If you'd built it further down the place would be flooded out, " she said, helping Hop-pity up.

" You'd best get back to bed, or you'll catch your death..."

"I probably would have if I hadn't fallen off the cloud," he grinned.

"I don't know, Rosy, tossing and turning half the night. You're falling out of bed," chuckled Cuckoo, "Now, try and get some sleep – I'll wake you at five, no six," he chirped, disappearing into his clock.

The thunder faded as it moved into the distance and finally the gentle sound of rain pattering on the grass above calmed Hop-pity and soothed them both back to sleep.

-:-

GOT YOU!

Hop-pity was looking for a friendly caterpillar amid the cabbages, but Rosy said that it had probably changed into a butterfly.

"Dr. Squirrel was telling me that Mr. Darwin's book 'Origins of the Species' explains how everything changes over many years, in a process known as evolution.

"Cyril agrees with Mr. Darwin, but said that caterpillars contradict the theory, as they transform themselves much, much too quickly! How they do it is a mystery — but the caterpillars, butterflies and moths won't give away their secret.

"He believes that caterpillars spin pupas to hide in. Then travel into the future for an operation leaving them with just six legs - and have wings stitched on with invisible thread so that they can fly. Then break out of their pupas as butterflies!

" He thinks you know about time travel, because you said after following a butterfly that waited for you on a flower in the park, before you arrived in the lake at Somerton Farm..! Did you know, he's been making mixtures of pupas, their silky interiors and other ingredients ever since he met you?

"Personally I think he's as mad as his Dad, who made wings from bird feathers, leapt off a cliff and drowned! That is why his Mum wanted him to be a doctor," she explained, frowned, put her finger to her lips and stared anxiously across the field.

"It's Farmer Beddows," she whispered, and ran, hiding behind Pogo the scarecrow.

Hop-pity knew that the farmer had seen them, but not wishing to give away Rosy's hiding place, he lowered his ears and crept between the cabbages hoping to get away across the meadow. But the farmer could see Hop-pity's tail and followed it.

—

" Got you!" he cried, grabbing hold of him, as Rosy watched Hop-pity struggling.

" Can you help him?" she asked Pogo.

" I'd help if I could but I've only one leg; if I had two I wouldn't be standing around here all day... Rabbits are more fortunate than me - having four legs they can run fast! Farmer Beddows made me, so I'm stuck here having to put up with the crows laughing at me," he moaned. " God designed you – but even Hop-pity isn't fast enough this time." Rosy winced and gave a deep sigh.

"Sorry," he apologised, "you're upset about your mate. I do wish I could help."

" But you can, Mr. Scarecrow. I am worried for Hop-pity's life – but I've a feeling our bunnies are due," she said, as they watched Shep the sheepdog spring into action.

He was chasing and jumping up at Farmer Beddows. They watched Hop-pity struggling to get free, while Shep the sheep dog tried to trip the farmer up.

" Get down, Shep" cried the farmer, but he kept chasing and leaping up until the farmer went into his cottage with Hop-pity, leaving Shep barking on the doorstep.

" Oh dear," cried Rosy, as Pogo tried to comfort her. "Not now of all times - our bunnies are going to be born and Hop-pity will never see them!" she sobbed,

"Shep! Shep come here, we need your help!" shouted Pogo, and catching sight of Rosy the dog raced towards them.

" Go, get Dr. Squirrel. Rosy's going to give birth," the scarecrow called, so Shep turned and ran off as fast as he could, but when they returned Rosy's bunnies had been born. Cyril Squirrel examined Rosy and the bunnies, congratulating her and Mr. Scarecrow on what a good job they'd done.

" You should be proud of yourself. You are doing very well, Rosy; but I'm afraid a field mouse has suffered a bad road accident, so I can't stop. How are you getting back to your burrow?" he enquired.

" Don't worry, I'll make sure Rosy gets home safely. We can carry one of the bunnies each with our mouth and I'm sure Mr. Scarecrow can look after the other one till I come back to collect him," said Shep.

" No need for that," responded Pogo, and throwing his hat to the ground he carefully lifted each of the bunnies into it.

" If you leave one of them with me he might get upset without his Mum. Do you think you can manage to carry them all in my new boater, between you?"

" What a good idea," said Dr. Squirrel, who was satisfied with the arrangement.

" Now, you and your family must all get some rest, Rosy. I'll call in to see you all tomorrow," he promised, leaving his patients in Shep's capable paws.

Rosy thanked Mr. Scarecrow for his help.

Pogo said that he'd never had so much excitement in his whole life – and that he'd look out for the bunnies when they were old enough to come and play in his field, because they were very, very special to him.

Rosy was both sad and happy, as she struggled along with Shep - finding the job very difficult, because Pogo had not considered Shep was taller than Rosy! The hat angling downwards as the pair tried to carry it between them, which caused the bunnies to rolled down and they were getting squashed.

Rosy and Shep put Pogo's boater full of bunnies down on the grass and overcame the problem with Shep doing the carrying while Rosy set the course and walking pace - as doctor Squirrel had said she must take things easy. Their new plan worked – Shep making sure that Rosy and her litter arrived home safely.

Shep's barking echoed through the burrow as he told Whistler everything that had happened, while Whistler set about making Rosy a refreshing cup of lemon mint tea.

"I'll go straight over to Big Brown Rabbit's, so that your Mum can look after everything for a few days," barked Shep, before reminding Rosy that Doctor Cyril Squirrel had said she must get some rest.

Shep met Rosy's parents near their burrow. He told them the bad and good news:

That Hop-pity had been caught by the farmer, then that they had become grandparents

They decided they should wait until the morning to see the bunnies and congratulate

Rosy, when Shep told them that Rosy was well but very tired.

It was true, Rosy was tired but she fed and bathed the bunnies. Rosy really missed

Hop-pity not being around, but she didn't feel quite so alone with her bunnies

snuggled around her in bed, and eventually they all curled up and fell fast asleep.

—

From Cumulus Nimbus, Father Time had been watching through his spyglass.

He'd seen the bunnies being born - and would have liked Hop-pity to see them too!

But he'd also seen Farmer Beddows catch Hop-pity and take him into his cottage.

Father Time decided Rosy, her family, Whistler and Pogo lived in the 19th century to

look after the bunnies, - and aware of Hop-pity's plight made the decision that it was

time for Hop-pity to advance into the 21st century, for his safety.

"Time flies," he ordered, tossing his scythe into the air! Glittering in the sunlight,

it span and wove a fascinating dance between the time pieces.

Autumn's leaves turned to snow, then rain. Petals from Spring's blossom fluttered

gently down. Summer rumbled, chimes and ticking fell silent as the time pieces

scurried from their master's path – freezing mid step as lightening forked.

Father Time appeared, seized his scythe and advanced slicing through the seasons

of a hundred and twenty-six calendars that marched against him. As he struck each

with a mighty blow, their splitting pages went flying over his shoulders and

disappeared into the past.

His work almost complete, he paused to wipe his brow using his scythe for

support. It turned in his hand, its sharp blade pointing at Farmer Beddows. Cottage.

From it a cascade of sparkling ice crystals glided like a sequinned comet, landing

with a pit-a-pat on the cottage roof, encircling the whole area with brightness.

" Hush," Father Time demanded. "The sands of time are passing! That's better -
the sands of the century are passing more quickly now." he smiled, as he listened -
his hour glass to his ear... Spring 2007 was returning...

—

Farmer Beddows was putting Hop-pity into a sack, when he suddenly paused
rubbing his aching legs, took off his hobnailed boots and rested in a chair by his fire.
Its glowing flames turned to embers, then ashes – his cottage roof started to leak.

Farmer Beddows' weathered face wrinkled and his dark brows turned grey, then
white. His plump cheeks paled sinking, leaving hollows. He shivered as a breeze
whistled around the room sending his hat flying off, whizzing, whirling to escape
through the open window. He too rose and went drifting after his hat like a smoke
trail, his outstretched arm reaching trying to retrieve it as he floated above the rapidly

changing landscape.

Down below, his view so strange

As greenery began to change.

Gone his shorthorn herd – and steer

As one by one farms disappear,

Allotments replace fields for hoeing, sowing.

Gone the calm of cattle mowing.

Hark! The wind of change is blowing.

—

Lucre lures the town-folk heither,

Via towering bridge they cross the river

To pasture – where huge steelwork's grow.

The woodland's axed. Proud mansions go!

Floating on, he stares aghast, at vast contrast

Steam engines, trams and tall ship masts,

Farmer and fields – lost to the past.

-:-

Hop-pity nibbled through the sack, struggled onto a work bench, but sprang down from the open window and ran, looking for Rosy among some cabbages. It was all very strange, he thought. Even Pogo had disappeared and Hop-pity had never seen Pogo move since the day Farmer Beddows had planted him.

He was rather confused as he sat down and noticed that the woodland, farms and stately mansions had disappeared too.... Yet the building and sounds of vehicles rushing by seemed somehow familiar - Suddenly Farmer Beddows' great-great grandson, Tom, grabbed hold of him.

"Got you at last! Everyone has been after you," he laughed.

-:-

NO GOING BACK.

Tom Beddow's took Hop-pity to his potting shed and put him into a box, tied it with string and carried it along the path to his van. He locked a seat belt safely around it, then got into the driver's seat and drove from his allotment at Somerton. He arrived at his destination, parked his van and went to the wool shop with captive Hop-pity – who was scared by the sound of the shop's bell and Tom Beddow's gruff voice as they entered...

" Good morning. How be the wool trade, Mrs. Jones? I reckon you'll be glad to know I've caught that rabbit we were looking for."

" Well done! You'll be wanting the reward then," replied Mrs. Jones.

" Wouldn't hear of it, but he 'aint 'arf led me a dance."

" *That woman wants to make me into an angora jumper - and they'll be laughing together as they're eating me in that rabbit pie on Sunday,*" Hop-pity whimpered.

"Thanks for the offer, but I work at my allotment Saturdays ready to sell stuff at the market on Sunday, so be there all day. I were digging up the spuds and stuff today, when this little rascal be scampering along a row of cabbage - could see his tail bouncing up and down like a cricket ball." he said, tapping the box.

" I were out working early - 'cause the rugby season starts today, guess that's why I caught him.

" Nothing gets in the way of rugby!" replied Mrs. Jones, picking up her telephone,

" Hello. Glad I've caught you..."

" *I wish the farmer hadn't caught me,*" Hop-pity sniffed.

" Yes... That's right... He's here at the wool shop ready for you to collect."

She must be talking to that butcher with the big knife, sobbed Hop-pity, as Mrs. Jones continued her conversation,

" Yes... all right, I'll expect you before I close at lunchtime, Sally."

Sally! *Is that my Sally she's talking to?* Wondered Hop-pity.

" At last I can remove the postcard I put in the shop window the day I met Sally outside Beechwood Park," smiled Mrs. Jones.

Hop-pity wiped his tears, listened and waited hopefully...

" Don't forget to put your clock forward tonight, Mrs. Jones!" Tom reminded her.

" I finish early on Saturdays too, so I might as well do it now." she said, picking her clock up, she turned it on the hour and left it on Hop-pity's box, while she went to remove the postcard from the shop window.

" That was quick, their car's just coming around the corner!" called Mrs Jones, who returned to put the clock back in its place before they arrived.

" I'm meeting my friends for the match, so I'd best be off... Hello Sal." smiled Mr. Beddow as he left.

On hearing the shop doorbell ring, *Hop-pity looked up, happy and very relieved to see Sally and her Dad peering down at him when the box was opened.* Sally took Hop-pity in her arms and they were soon on the way home, where he found himself back in his cosy rabbit hutch munching lettuce and gnawing at a carrot.

—

A few weeks passed. Today the garden was quiet except for a bee buzzing about pollinating as it collected nectar from the flowers. Birds twittered in the hedge and a grasshopper chirped in competition as silently the other insects went about their business.

One of those was a spider suspended from a silvery thread, blowing in a slight breeze, just outside Hop-pity's hutch. It swung across to a nearby rose bush and back again several times. Hop-pity was watching it busily spinning and weaving in and out from the centre - when a white butterfly flew over his hutch and perched on a bush of purple flowers in the garden.

" What are you doing? – Sally's Mum puts that lavender into little bags and hangs them in her wardrobes to keep moths out," called Hop-pity.

Butterfly looked up, he didn't know who was speaking but recognised the voice. It looked about but couldn't see anyone in the garden except for something moving about in what he took to be a big wooden box. Butterfly flew over to investigate and landing on the wire mesh window of the rabbit hutch looked in.

" Is that you Hop-pity?"

" Yes," Hop-pity replied.

" We've all been really worried – to be honest we've been more than worried – we thought you must be dead! When Farmer Beddows caught and took you off, we thought he'd taken you to the wool shop. Did they put you in this prison cell?"

" Prison, this is not a prison! Its my hutch. I'm very comfortable living here," replied Hop-pity defensively. What business is it of yours – I don't think I even know you! "

" Yes you do, I'm Caterpillar that lived in Scarecrow's cabbage field. In those days I used to dream that I could fly – now look at me, aren't my new wings beautiful?" Butterfly was showing off as it fluttered about.

" Yes, yes, you look lovely," nodded Hop-pity. " but do be careful, you don't want to get too near that spider's web."

" Oh dear! Good job you warned me, after my wonderful transformation I could have come to a sticky end… You still don't remember me, do you?"

" If you are the caterpillar I remember, you certainly have changed! Did you used to have black and yellow stripes – and were you furry like a bee but your stripes went from your neck right down your back?"

" Yes that was me, then – but look at me now."

" It's no wonder I didn't recognise you… If I hadn't followed a butterfly that looked just like you I'd have never lived in the woods at Beechwood with you all.

" You might have followed my Mum – Pogo said I look like her. I never met her myself. I only remember living in his cabbage field – I guess my Mum left me in Mr. Scarecrow's field knowing I'd have plenty to eat there. She knew that Pogo would look after me, making sure I wouldn't be eaten by the birds. She must have loved me very much, Hop-pity… Mr. Scarecrow explained that she was getting old and wouldn't have survived the cold winter weather, so he looked after me instead."

" Rosy said you'd turn into a butterfly – and a very beautiful one too – if I may say so! I wasn't sure whether to believe her, but it seems she was right. Is Rosy alright?"

" She's been rather busy, but she is fine. I can't wait to tell her that I've seen you," it said, spreading its wings.

" Hey, wait a minute – Tell her I'm living back in my cosy hutch and that Sally is looking after me. Then she'll know I'm alright too."

" Okay, but I must get off to give everyone the good news, Hop-pity."

" Be careful! You'll keep in touch, won't you?" called Hop-pity, as the butterfly took to the sky. He watched it fluttering into the distance until he could see it no longer.

The spider frowned, wondering if building a web between Hop-pity's hutch and the rose bush had been such a good idea – if Hop-pity was going to warn the flies not to get caught in its web. Hop-pity rather enjoyed the spider's company so assured it that his rather smelly toilet area of the hutch attracted flies but he hated the flies coming in to the toilet area and then onto his food in his living room. The spider told Hop-pity that he preferred flies to eat because they didn't flap their wings about like butterflies which meant he had fat juicy meals without having to keep rebuilding the web. So they were both happy, because they would be doing each other a favour

The following day Sally caught a glimpse of a hedgehog before it scampered beneath the hedge.

Hop-pity had heard Sally's Dad telling her that hedgehogs were good for the garden, because they ate slugs and that he hoped the hedgehog would live under their hedge. The next time Hop-pity saw the hedgehog he told him that he was most welcome to stay with in Sally's garden.

Hedgehog replied, that his wife had died when she had been run over by a motor cycle in a nasty accident and had been feeling very lonely ever since. He was intrigued to hear that Hop-pity was caught hiding among cabbages, how the woodland where he'd lived, his friends and wife Rosy had all disappeared - like a bad dream.

After their conversation Hedgehog felt happier, knowing he wasn't the only one feeling lonely. He understood that Rosy meant as much to Hop-pity as Mrs. Hedgehog had meant to himself. Therefore he happily agreed to accept the family's kind invitation to stay and set to work building a new home in Sally's garden.

When he had settled in Hop-pity and Hedgehog talked a lot about problems and discovered that having someone to talk things over with helped a lot. Their tears soon turned to smiles, which resulted in a friendship that was very special indeed.

-:-

SALLY'S TALE.

" Morning, did you sleep well?"

Hop-pity was surprised to be waking to the sound of Sally's voice! He glanced around his old hutch. The events of Farmer Beddows catching him and the wool shop came flooding back although he felt relief at seeing Sally looking down at him.

—

"I couldn't sleep last night for thinking of you – I'm so excited that you're home again. I can hardly believe you are really here... Dad made some improvements to your hutch while you were away. Look, the door is hinged at the bottom instead of at the side - now it drops forward so it works like a draw bridge on an old castle," Sally explained. "You can use it as your very own pathway down to the lawn – Isn't that clever, Hop-pity? It's much safer too, now that it locks with a bolt at the top so you won't ever get lost again!" she smiled.

Hop-pity examined where Sally's Dad had removed the old hinges, and nodded.

" I got out of bed and looked down at you sleeping from my bedroom window, last night as, if I were the Man in the Moon. But the moon wasn't looking down at me – there was a crab on the moon, it looked like a hermit crab- stretching out its claw trying to reach the Man who was on the other side! It must be lonely living up there all alone. Perhaps it was trying to cheer the Man up because he couldn't see us – like the night when I came back from the seaside and couldn't find you, Hop-pity. That night I asked The Man in the Moon to look out for you."

Hop-pity wanted to say that the moon's face looked like Sally's Dad, but twitched his nose, aware that animals never talk to humans - and it would be rude to interrupt!

"I'd been looking at little creatures in rock pools and collecting shells when a crab came from under the rocks, and walked sideways along the beach. That was the day I lost you – but found the biggest shell I've ever seen, - it was amazing – I couldn't bring it home to show you, but I'll tell you about it..."

-:-

"Dad was tired after driving, so I helped him move our deckchairs back because the tide was coming in. He pointed out the Ice Cream Parlour so I'd know where they were sitting and allowed me to go exploring all on my own -while he and Mum had a rest.

"At the end of the beach there were cliffs. I went rock pooling and climbed down into a cove, picked up some pebbles and tried skimming them across the water. I was hopeless at it so I gave up– but that's when I found this cave!

"It was cold and dark inside. I shouted Hello! But the echo that came back said…

" Hello, here I am -I am. Over here -here!"

"I knew it couldn't be **my** voice echoing, so thought, there must be somebody else there." Then I heard the voice again.

" I'm here –here. Please find me –me," it echoed around the cave...

" It was scary. Then I thought it must be a little girl wanting to play Hide and Seek, so I followed the sound of her voice, straining my eyes looking for her, and suddenly came across an enormous, beautiful blue shell. The girl's voice seemed to be coming from inside. I knocked and asked if she was hiding inside."

" I'm not hiding in my shell – I sleep in it!" she answered " I was asleep, when the sea picked it up - and I have no idea where it's taken me. -This sort of thing can happen if too much air gets trapped inside... I can't understand why I hear the water rolling pebbles, a heavy battering, the pebbles moving again, then everything becomes quiet for hours. – I can only guess that I must be at a place where the tide turns."

" I told her she was in a cave and that her shell was firmly wedged between the wall of the cave and a rock."

"That would explain it," she said and began to sob.

" I told her that I'd go and get my Dad. - but she argued there wouldn't be time and begged me not to leave her. She'd been trapped for almost a week and said if she didn't get away on the next tide she'd probably die!"

-:-

Hop-pity was concerned – remembering how he had felt locked in a box when Tom Beddow had taken him to the wool shop. He recalled planning his escape to Holland with Cyril Squirrel to avoid Farmer Beddows' gun - knowing that Holland was by the sea – but had never actually seen the sea. Hop-pity was extremely interested – but perhaps a bit confused about Sally's words.

" She asked me to hurry, collect seaweed and rub it on her shell where it was wedged to loosen it."

" I did and as the seaweed bubbles popped, they released a slimy liquid, that made the shell very slippery," Sally explained.

" Then I put my back against the shell and levered myself up the wall of the cave with my feet making a humpback bridge across the gap. The shell hinge dug into my back. I winch from the pain as I forced my knees down with both hands to straighten them as I pushed against the shell. Suddenly - the shell shot out, and I fell backward banging my head on the rock!

" When I came to my senses I discovered the girl - was a mermaid! She was pouring salt water on my head and smarting back saying that the salt would heal the cut – she was a mermaid, I tell you. She had a big scaly fish tail and long dark hair. Everything about her was like the mermaid I'd read about in a story at school.

" When she knew I was okay, she rolled over into the sea. It had come lapping over the pebbles. into the cave. I struggled back onto my feet.

" Well done, you managed it in time," she cheered - " but I was worried. The water rising so quickly, you understand. I began wading through it - only then I realised just how far I'd gone into the cave following the mermaid's voice.

"She was wallowing about, happily munching seaweed - I was terrified – the water had climbed up my legs and still flooding into the cave. As it reached my waist, the waves were hitting the back of the cave. My feet were being dragged this way and that, causing me to lose balance. I didn't know what to do. Tumbling about I shouted to let the mermaid know I was in trouble and couldn't swim."

Hop-pity was listening to every word, trying to imagine it, as Sally continued.
" The waves started splashing up into my face as they broke, then smashed against the rocks before hustling back again. It was dreadful...

"We're trapped!" I shouted.

"No we're not, trust me. Get on my back and hold tight."

" I did as she'd instructed, grabbing hold of her hair - just as another wave hit with great force, carrying us back. She threw her tail up, dived and swung around before we smashed into rocks at the back of the cave. I went right under the water, holding my breath and hung on like a limpet – came back to the surface and took a big breath as we were chased by a returning wave that pushed towards the entrance. I couldn't catch up with her. It was so exciting, but turned scary – when two waves collided. As they crashed I was thrown -almost hitting the ceiling, then splashed down kicking and spluttering, beneath the waves. She was round, through my legs and back up to the surface in seconds

" Finding myself on her back I grabbed her hair and she was off ducking and diving over waves carrying me out of the cave. She was so strong - I wish I could swim like that, Hop-pity! Once we were outside she went surfing along the waves. Seagulls squealed, applauding as she went leaping over the foaming breakers, crashing as they rolled over, raced forward, washing and rippling onto the sand.

" Then the mermaid paused, flapping her tale in the shallows as I slipped off her back and paddled my way back onto the beach. I turned to wave but then sprang to catch this comb she threw to me, instead.

"Here, keep my comb to remember me - I owe you my life!" she called, diving beneath the waves. I caught her comb and scoured the waves… She was gone!"

-:-

"Look, it's no ordinary comb," Sally said, urging Hop-pity to look. " It's shaped like a seahorse –it teeth down its tummy"

Hop-pity squinted through his netted window A horse with teeth in its tummy, he frowned. The only horses I know live in the stables at Somerton Farm, they have four legs and their teeth in their mouths like me! They certainly don't look like that, he though, sniffing at Sally's comb through the netting - and decided that a seahorse comb was not something to be eaten. He gave Sally a pleading look, wondering when she was going to feed him.

"Mum and Dad said I couldn't have been with a mermaid because they don't exist, but I'm sure they do - because I've got her comb to prove it!" Sally grinned, filling Hop-pity's water bottle. Then she put a carrot and fresh lettuce into his hutch, asking:

"Do you think she was a real mermaid?"

Hop-pity was rather puzzled - confused about caves, seaweed, waves, mermaids, not to mention seahorses - so pondered a moment before making his decision. - Had this really happened the day he'd followed the butterfly, he wondered, remembering the Maindee houses, farms, woodlands and the friends he'd made while living their.

I suppose it may have, he though, considering what Rosy's answer would be –

" Well – Maybe, maybe not!" - he smiled, bringing back all the excitement and marvellous memories of his Wedding Day - the happiest day of his life..! His

wonderful daydream was to be disturbed by Sally's Mum calling,

" What are you up to, Sally? Hurry up or you'll be late for school!"

Sally ran back to the house. So Hop-pity decided it was time to get on with his

breakfast.

FROM TIME TO TIME.

Hop-pity had leapt forward to the year 2007. Rosy lived back in 1880 the span of years between made it impossible for them to ever met again.

In the February Dr. Squirrel had woken feeling rather hungry, but only had one apple left, he braved the cold, dug up some acorns that he'd buried in Autumn and set about making himself a nice apple and acorn soup. He washed and prepared the fruit, added a few icicles to the ingredients - but needing to know how long to cook it – climbed up to an alcove to get his Mum's old cookery book. Butterfly flew into his home and began circling around Cyril's head making him feel quite dizzy - causing him to drop the book. It fell, knocking a box containing a collection of chrysalis, silk, dried stingy nettles, cabbage, clover, violet and privet leaves. off the shelf.

" Now look what you've done!" he shouted, bending to clean up the mess.

Sorry, Doctor," Butterfly apologised " but my visit is important! I've seen Hop-pity. He asked me to tell everyone that he is alive and well!"

" Where is he?" asked the doctor, eyeing Butterfly suspiciously.

" He's living in Sally's garden, in the hutch he told us about."

" You shouldn't be about in February, so **exactly when,** did you see him? queried Cyril, considering a possible connection between Hop-pity's sighting by a Cabbage White butterfly, that to his knowledge, had recently emerged from being a caterpillar!

" Ah! Well, can't say," replied Butterfly.

" I am his doctor and I have a right to visit my patient and make sure he wasn't harmed by Farmer Beddows," Cyril insisted.

" But I just told you he is alright!"

"That's not really good enough. You know very well what I'm asking, don't you?"

Butterfly nodded, as a yellow dust falling from its antenna which floated, then frothed as it sizzled in Cyril's soup.

Not wishing to cause Cyril further distress, Butterfly hastily flew from Cyril's oak

tree as fast as it could, knowing that he would want answers to further question about

secrets that he had taken an oath to never disclose."

"Hum! I knew it," muttered Cyril, "Hop-pity did know the secret of time travel!

Now I'll never learn their secret, " he sulked. "Never mind, my soup smells good,

even though I didn't put all the ingredients in – thanks to that annoying butterfly." He

groaned, and tasted it for flavour, unaware that oddments from his strange collection

had fallen into his soup.

"Yuck! What is that?" He frowned, and pulling a face at its not so pleasant smell,

looked at the bits and bobs frothing on the top of it. "I'm not eating that!" he

shouted, and picking up the saucepan carried it to his entrance and threw all the soup

out. His soup sank into the soil.

He stamped about swinging his saucepan about in annoyance, causing an acorn to

fall into the soupy soil. It immediately rooted itself and began to suck up Cyril's soup

- which had a very strange effect on the soil around the little acorn.

Directly beneath the soupy soil Big Brown Rabbit was digging an extension,

because Rosy's burrow needed an extra bedroom for her bunnies.

Big Brown Rabbit had hollowed out the soil for the bedroom, but was puzzled by

a smell, damp patches and tiny roots pushing their way through the walls that he was

trying neatly to smooth down. For this reason he dug alongside a root, following it

to see what was causing the trouble. As it turned upwards, he dug upwards, surfaced

and poked his head out- shocked to discover that he had no idea where he was!

He ran back down the burrow and looked out through Rosy's entrance to find that

everything looked normal, except that an acorn had recently started to grow above the bedroom he'd been working on. He scampered back long Rosy's burrow, through

the bedroom and along the narrow passageway he'd dug, and looked out again.

He couldn't understand it, nothing like this had ever happened before – and he'd built

many - very many burrows!

"Rosy, come and have a look at this!" he shouted.

" What's wrong, Dad?" she called, rushing into the new bedroom.

"Phew! What ever has happened? she sniffed, "Where are you, Dad?"

" In the corner of the bedroom you'll find a passageway – Come and see!"

" What's he dug that for?" she tutted. "I didn't need that," but she followed it and

pushed her head through the hole, and saw Big Brown Rabbit – his front paws against,

an oak as he stretched peering down over a city, a number of bridges **now** spanning a

familiar river. Rubbing his eyes, he stared **in disbelief** recognising the skyline, two

islands in a channel beyond the river and the distant coastline.

Rosy was staring at houses across a road, which were tiny compared to the lovely

Maindee mansions.

"Where are we, Dad?"

" We haven't come far to get here, so must still be near your burrow. Things have

changed somehow. Look at the river, coast and skylines – even Flat and Steep Holm

islands are here," he pointed, " The humans have been busy doing all this – I simply

can't understand how they chopped the woodland down without us knowing about it."

They quickly took cover behind the oak tree, when they heard footsteps and a voice

–

"Sally, you'd better put Hop-pity back in his hutch now. Come on, your lunch

is getting cold. – Hurry up, you'll have to be off to school again soon."

Big Brown Rabbit looked at Rosy – Rosy's eyes filled with tears, her mouth gaping as she stared back at her Dad. They stayed hid behind an oak tree until Sally left for school with her Mum.

Then they squeezed beneath the nearby fence and began to run beneath where juicy black grapes hung, supported by a plum tree. They sprang onto steps and bounced down excitedly, to where they found a rabbit hutch at the edge of a lawn.

—

Rosy gasped, on seeing who was asleep in the hutch, her Dad clawed at the window netting, disturbing Hop-pity, who dreaming about Rosy, closed his eyes again. The pair of them began beating their paws hard against the hutch till they shook him awake.

Hop-pity was amazed at seeing them. He told them the lady from the wool shop had no intention of making wool from his fur or making rabbit pie. She only wanted to return him to Sally - his rightful owner, who had been worried and very unhappy since losing him – which he understood from missing Rosy so much.

Hop-pity explained that his friend Hedgehog was hibernating, and that on Sundays Sally visited her Grandma. They went to Christchurch Church, passing Beechwood where he'd lived with Rosy, Whistler and his friends. He said he was sad on Sundays, being all alone until Monday because Sally's family didn't get home until suppertime.

" I'll come and see you on Sunday," Rosy smiled.

—

The following Sunday Rosy and three bunnies squeezed under a fence, and ran down to Sally's lawn.

" Surprise, surprises!" they shouted.

" Are they ours?" he asked. Rosy nodded. " That's why you were seeing Dr. Squirrel," he laughed.

"Yes, but they can only come on Sundays! The roads are far too busy here, where you live, and we wouldn't want an accident, would we?" Hop-pity agreed.

"It's wonderful. They're wonderful!" Hop-pity grinned, proudly beaming with joy. So it was arranged that Rosy, or her parents, would bring the bunnies to see Hop-pity every Sunday to spend time playing in Sally's garden with him. Rosy was happy again and so was Pogo who organised games of Hide and Seek for the bunnies to play in his cabbage field.

Whistler was glad to hear that Hop-pity was happy as the cow that jumped over the moon to see Rosy and his bunnies every week – safe from Farmer Beddow's gun! I'm not sure what Big Brown Rabbit thought of Whistler being 'Best Rabbit' in Hop-pity's absence. – but it certainly made Whistler feel a very important part of the Brown Rabbit's family when they called in for tea.

Dr. Cyril Squirrel never realised that by throwing away his horrible tasting soup, he'd accidentally succeeded in finding the way for Rosy's family to time travel. That remained a mystery to everyone – accept for you, me and Big Brown Rabbit's family!

One day great celebrations could be heard when a park for the people was opened. That day Rosy found a newspaper with a picture of an aeroplane in it when returning from visiting Hop-pity. She asked Pigeon the Post to deliver it to Cyril - but he was out trying to discover what all the fuss was about. Brass bands could be heard, then a balloon blew across the river, got caught up in a railway engine's steam, it chugged along after it until a cross wind blew it up the hill. Cyril sprang from a tree, grasped a string attached to the strange object and went sailing through the air – but it landed in the duck pond with a splash! Cyril arrived home wet and bedraggled, found the newspaper and believed that his, best friend, Hop-pity had sent it from the 21st Century. He was so pleased that he stopped asking butterflies about time travel and took up a new hobby: Dr. Cyril Squirrel spent the rest of his life trying to building an aeroplane!

THE END.

99.

Story / Poem.	Topic Options.
1. Little White Rabbit.	Pets and Garden Wild life.
2. Easter Surprise.	Seasons and Celebrations. Minutes and hours.
3. Hop-pity's Hutch.	Man made construction / Straight edged shapes
4. Cracking The Code	Communication: Sign, Braille, Mail, Bell, Internet
5. Hop-pity Goes Exploring.	Farm Animals / Day and Night / Draw rabbit's trip
6. Hop-pity Makes A Move.	Homes.(Strength of curved burrows.) ½ and ¼
7. Sally's Shadow.	Time. Space and why Earth has Seasons
8. The Intruder.	Telling the Time and 5 times table.
9. Clever Clogs.	Mirror Image. Water-windmill/electricity.
10. Catkins or Lambs Tail	Flower, pollination, fruit, seed.
11. Sally's Search.	Primary colours/Rainbows and colour mixing.
12. Litter Lout.	Hygiene. Country Code, Laws, School Rules.
13. A Narrow Escape.	Bees and their Hives.
14. Hop-pity	Farming. Animals supply our needs
15. Jennie The Donkey.	Working Animals/birds. Autumn Hibernation.
16. Pot of Gold.	Migration. Russia, Holland in Europe. Plague.
17. Rhyme and Reason.	Roman battle/building. 10, 9 and 11 times table
18. Hop-pity in Love	Submersibles. Making Cards/envelope/boxes.
19. Hop-pity's Birthday.	Birth and growth / 12 months, days in months.
20. Maybe May Day.	Chains/mechanics. Making decisions and plans.
21. A Day to Remember.	Spinning, weaving, dying. Maypole Dance. Fire.
22. Friend and Neighbour.	Talking to strangers. Winter Hexagons.
23. The Meadow Mystery.	The Water Cycle. Magnification.
24. Cumulus Nimbus.	Climate Change. Stars / kites. The library.
25. Got You.	Metamorphosis. Helping each other. Change.
26. No Going Back.	The Food Chain. Pests and Predators.
27. Sally's Tale.	Sea creatures, fossils, skeleton design, Holidays.
28. From Time To Time.	Family, Judging people and choosing friends,.

Sally received Hop-pity in the year 2005. He vanished to reappear in 1879. They were separated by time until reunited in 2008. Yet both lived in Newport the town that Her Majesty Queen Elizabeth II granted city status in order to mark the new Millennium.

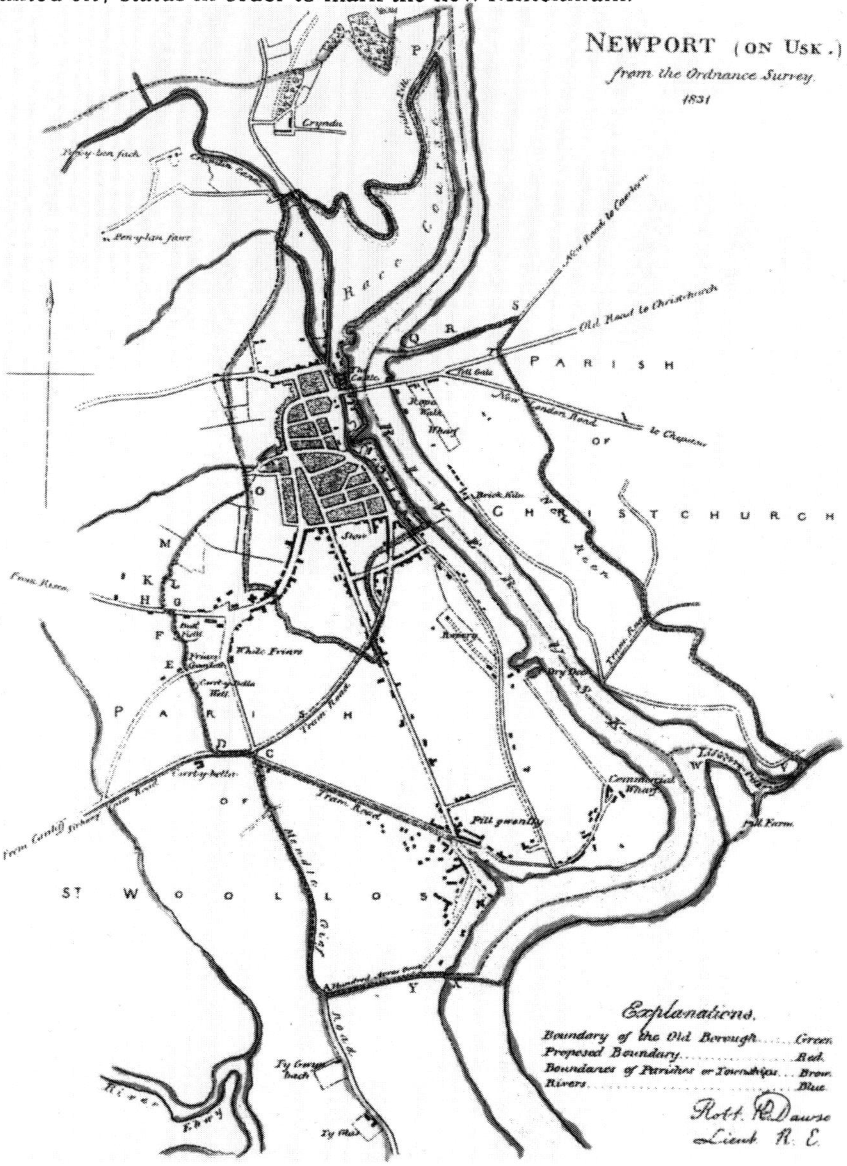

1831 – Newport, situated West of the River Usk. The map shows proposed boundary extension: South to 100 Acres Gout and East into Christchurch Parish - to the junction of Caerleon and Christchurch Roads.

Like Newport, this land was owned by the Rt. Hon. Visct. Tredegar. - Whose ancestor: The buccaneer of Captain Morgan's Rum fame - was knighted and made deputy-governor of Jamaica on the 23rd Jan. 1674, by Charles II.
-:-

NEWPORT (ON USK.)
from the Ordnance Survey
1831

Lord Herbert of Cherbury: owned the land North of the East boundary along the river, known as St. Julian's (the place of martyrdom of Julius during the Roman occupation) as far as Caerleon.

The name **Caerleon** originates from its Roman title **Castra Legion**is where the 2nd Roman Legion was based. Its Roman Baths, amphitheatre, pottery and barracks for the Legion's 6,000 soldiers - hovels for the Silurian slaves.
-:-

LORD HERBERT of CHERBURY.

South of Lord Herbert's land stood:

The Maendy Estate

(Maendy is Welsh, meaning: House of stones. Later to be re-spelt Maindee)

In 1615 Sir Charles Somerset, 6th son of the Earl of Worcester sold Maendy Estate, to John Rosser of Caerleon. It was inherited by his son, William and sold in 1848.

Sale Details. ➔

The value of the estate made obvious by the footnote: Plans and particulars available at Newport, Bath, Cardiff, Bristol. Garraway's Coffee House, plus three other London addresses.

Wm. Kemeys purchased Maindee Estate. I understand that Eve's Well and Fair Oak farms were rented

MAINDEE ESTATE.

SECOND DAY'S SALE.

The Particulars and Conditions of Sale
OF
VERY VALUABLE ESTATES,
Freehold and Copyhold of Inheritance,
MOST DELIGHTFULLY SITUATE, CHIEFLY ON
A SOUTH & SOUTH-WESTERN BANK,
COMMANDING
Extensive and highly diversified Views,
INCLUDING
THE BRISTOL CHANNEL, THE TOWN & PORT OF NEWPORT,
AND
THE MONMOUTHSHIRE AND GLAMORGAN HILLS,
NOW FORMING
THE FAIR OAK, EVE'S WELL, AND PEN Y LAN FARMS,
In the Parish of CHRISTCHURCH, and County of MONMOUTH.
AND ONLY ABOUT
A MILE FROM THE TOWN OF NEWPORT,
WHICH WILL BE DIVIDED
In suitable Lots for erecting Villa Residences.

Which will be Sold by Auction,
BY MESSRS.

FAREBROTHER, CLARK & LYE

At the King's Head Hotel, Newport,
On WEDNESDAY, the 16th of AUGUST, 1848,
AT ONE O'CLOCK, IN FORTY-EIGHT LOTS.

To be Viewed, and Particulars with Plans had of Mr. Morris, Surveyor, Newport; White Lion, Bristol; White Horse, Bath; Cardiff Arms, Cardiff; of Messrs. Baker and Co., Solicitors, No. 52, Lincoln's-inn-fields, London; of Messrs. Downes, Gamlen and Scott, Solicitors, No. 7, Furnival's-inn, London; at Garraway's Coffee House; and at the Offices of Messrs. FAREBROTHER, CLARK & LYE, No. 6, Lancaster Place, Strand, London.

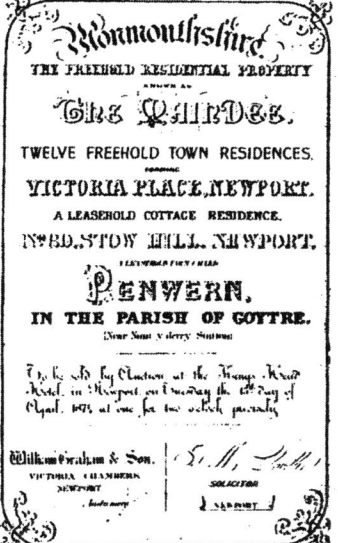

⬅ until his whole estate was sold by auction, in 1774.

The Maindee, divided into lesser lots, sold to four gentlemen.

Fair Oak and Eves Well Farms, were bought by: land agent, Wm. Graham and solicitor, Henry Farr. The map dated 1853 seems to confirm that Fair Oak Farm had been rented from Wm. Kemeys.- with an agreement allowing them to divide the farm into allotments for subletting to Newport's townsfolk. (Map 2.)

The shrewd businessmen collected rent from the custodians of each allotment and laid streets (N.B. Victoria and Albert joined by the crown) - aware that the land's value would increase to accommodate the population growth of Newport. As they had anticipated the borough boundary was extended further. (See terraced houses at edges of map 3.) Map 2.

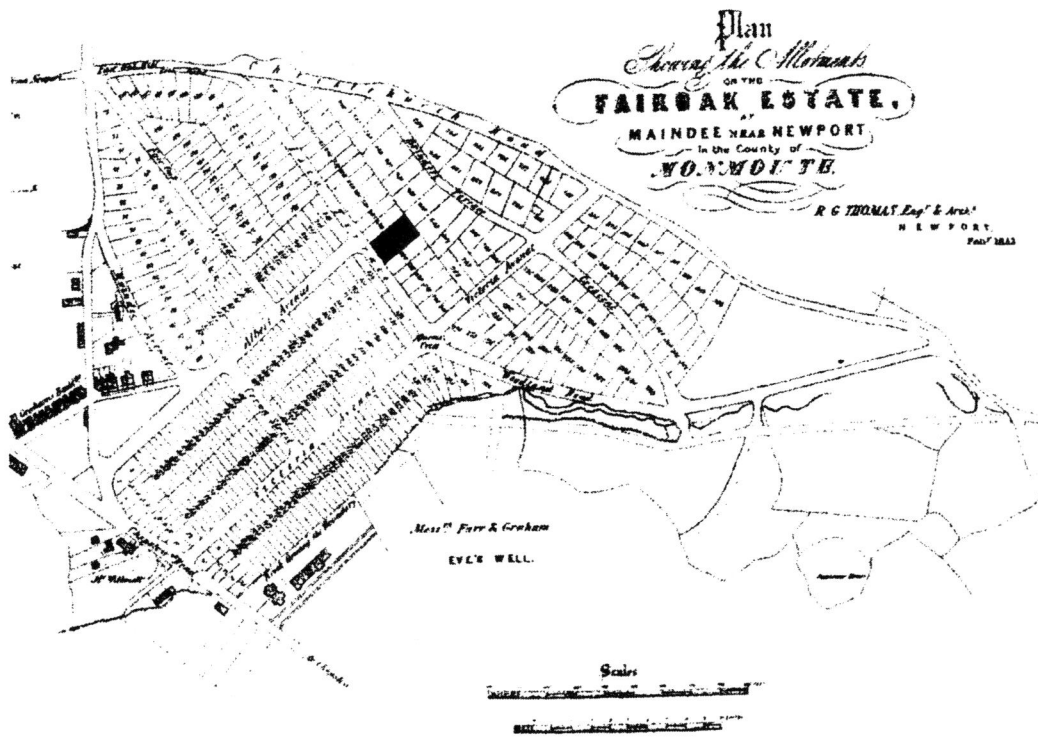

Railway and canal engineer, John. Logan, bought Lot 1: Maindee Mansion, plus Somerton Farm and 369 acres of Spitty/Lliswerry grazing land for his prize winning shorthorn cattle. Canal engineering contractor James Rennie purchased Pen-Y-Lan Farm, and raised revenue by following Graham and Farr's example to build Maindee Park and allowed his brother land to build Maindee Hall. Had it not been for Logan and Rennie the setting for Hop-pity's adventures would have never materialised.

Lot 1. Maindee Mansion gives some indication of how the stately homes would have been viewed by the townsfolk living across the river.

Built by wealthy gentlemen, the mansions of Hatherleigh, Beechwood and others nestled between hillside trees as long horned cattle grazed at the riverside meadows, backdrop to where sails drifted along the Usk. In contrast were canal and dock labourers clad in rags and coal dust. Beggars starved.

-:-

Map 3 shows The Maindee Mansion at the base. Maindee Hall and Maindee Park central. At the top, Gaer (i.e. fort) Wood, the Roman - later Roundhead's - Camp and well.

Particulars.

LOT 1.
"THE MAINDEE,"

Situate upon the Turnpike Road leading to Chepstow, one mile from the thriving and populous Borough and Port of Newport, and a quarter-of-an-hour's drive from First-class Railway Stations, giving access to all parts of the Kingdom; it is a Residence suitable for a Merchant or Manufacturer rarely to be found in the Market.

THE PLEASURES OF THE CHASE may be enjoyed with Two Packs of Fox Hounds, which meet within an easy distance several days in the week.

GOOD SALMON AND TROUT FISHING are to be obtained in the River Usk, so celebrated for the superiority of its Fish.

There is a CHURCH within half-a-mile.

THE MANSION,

Built about Fifteen Years ago of Bath Stone, upon the site of the original Mansion, is a plain but substantial Structure, replete with costly Fittings.

The Entrance Front has a Westerly aspect, and you pass through a Porch to the following Rooms :—

On the Ground Floor : A Hall, 18 ft. 6 in. by 12 ft., with Floor of Mosaic Pavement ; Library, 18 ft. by 12 ft. Morning Room, 18 ft. 6 in. by 17 ft. 6 in.

Dining and Drawing Rooms, each 22 ft. by 18 ft. 6 in., and all 12 ft. in height.

The Domestic Offices comprise Large Kitchen, Scullery, Butler's Pantry, Cook's Pantry, Dairy, Larder, Wash-house, and Laundry ; and in the

Basement are capacious Wine and Beer Cellars,

FROM AN INNER HALL SPRINGS

AN EASY STONE STAIRCASE,

Well lighted, and giving access to Six Best Bed Chambers, One Dressing Room, Bath Room, and W.C.

The BED ROOMS are of the following dimensions—

North Front (1 Room)	15 ft. 0 in. by 15 ft.	West Front (3 Rooms)	22 ft. by 18 ft.
East „ (1 Room)	13 ft. 6 in. by 13 ft.		22 ft. by 18 ft.
South „ (1 Room)	18 ft. 6 in. by 13 ft.		19 ft. by 12 ft.
	All 12 ft. high.		

A SECONDARY STAIRCASE leads to Three Servants Bed Rooms and an Attic.

THE RESIDENCE

Is approached from the Turnpike Road through a pair of elegant Iron Gates, (flanked by an Ornamental Lodge) along a Carriage Drive, belted with a row of large and stately Elm Trees, to the Lawns and Pleasure Grounds. These are laid out with great taste, are well furnished with rare and costly Trees and Shrubs, and are adorned by a Fountain, through which flows a Stream of Water, scattering its spray over the Ornamental Foliage around.

THE KITCHEN GARDENS

Are conveniently situate, with an approach through a charming little parterre, are well walled in, and planted with choice Fruit Trees. There is a large VINERY, a range of FORCING PITS, FRUIT HOUSE, and an ORCHARD.

THE STABLE DEPARTMENT

Is placed at a convenient distance from the Mansion, and comprises standing for Four Carriages, Four Stalls, and One Loose Box ; Loft, Harness Room, and Coachman's House.

The whole surrounded, except on the North-east side (where the Turnpike Road leading from Newport to Chepstow is the boundary), by 10 Acres of rich MEADOW LAND.

Just below lies a wood - where few trees remain today - from whence a squirrel leaves an oak tree to visit the author's garden. In Summer it breaks bird feeders and steals fruit. In Autumn it buries acorns, but fails to eat them all - leaving the author to uproot oak saplings from her garden through Spring! She lives midway between Beechwood and Eveswell Parks, that is why she has plenty of wildlife characters to write about.

-:-

Map 3

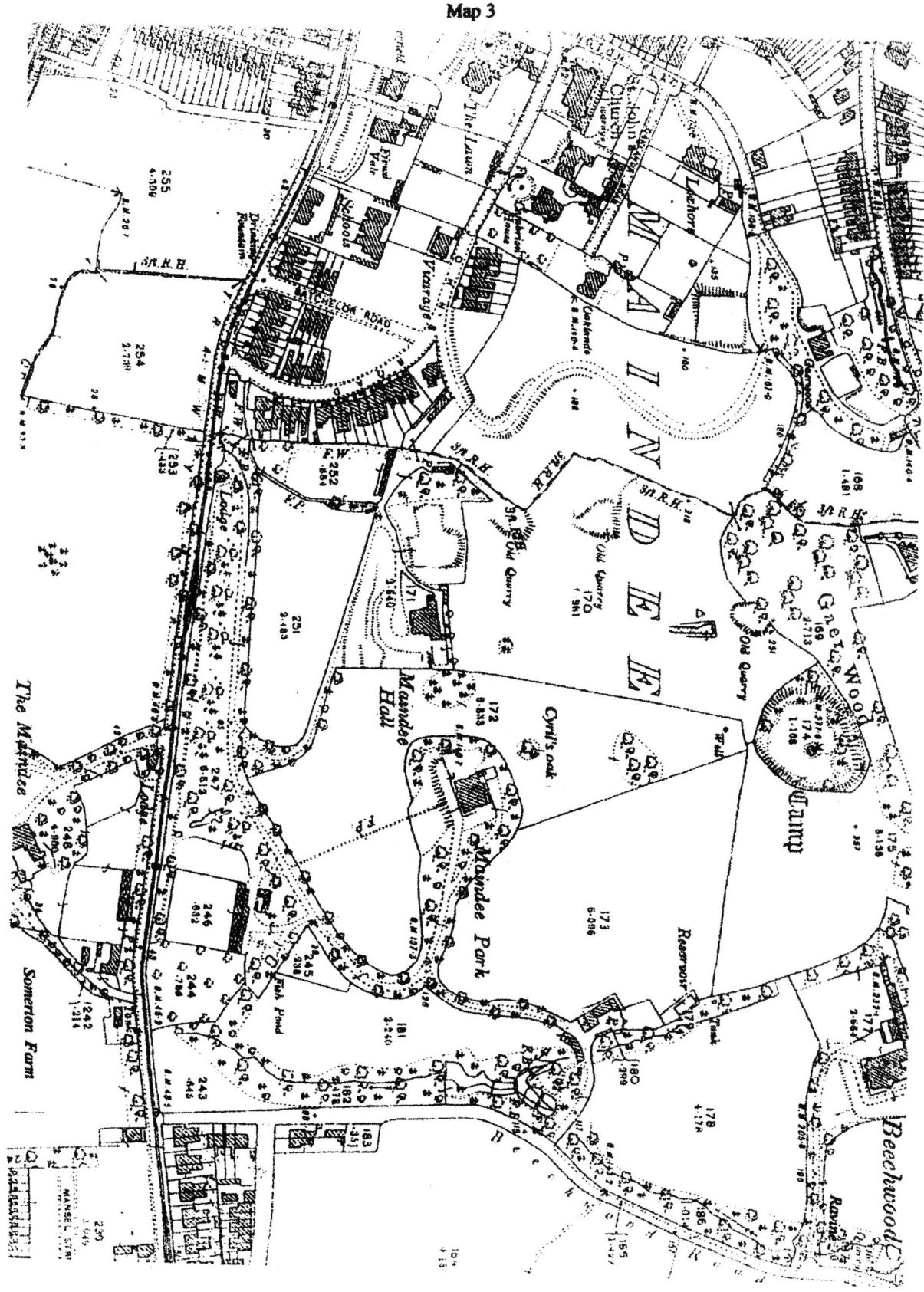

The front view of 'The Maindee'.

Maindee Park. Photograph published in 1892.

The main gates of 'The Maindee' which fronted Chepstow Road opposite the present day gates of Beechwood Park.

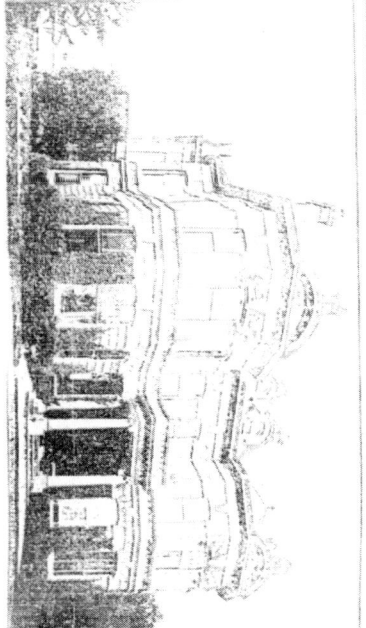

SALE OF MANSION & LANDS
KNOWN AS
"MAINDEE HALL,"

AT THE

Westgate Hotel, Newport, on Wednesday, June 29, 1898

AT 3 P.M.

MAP 4.
1901.

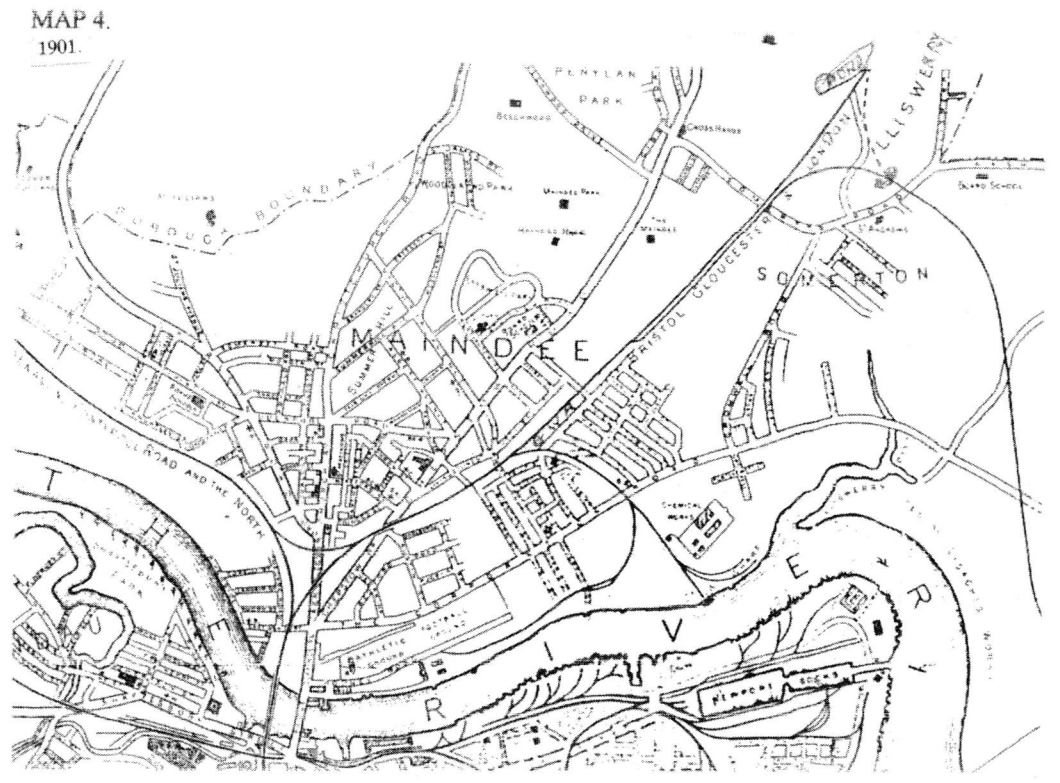

Map 5.

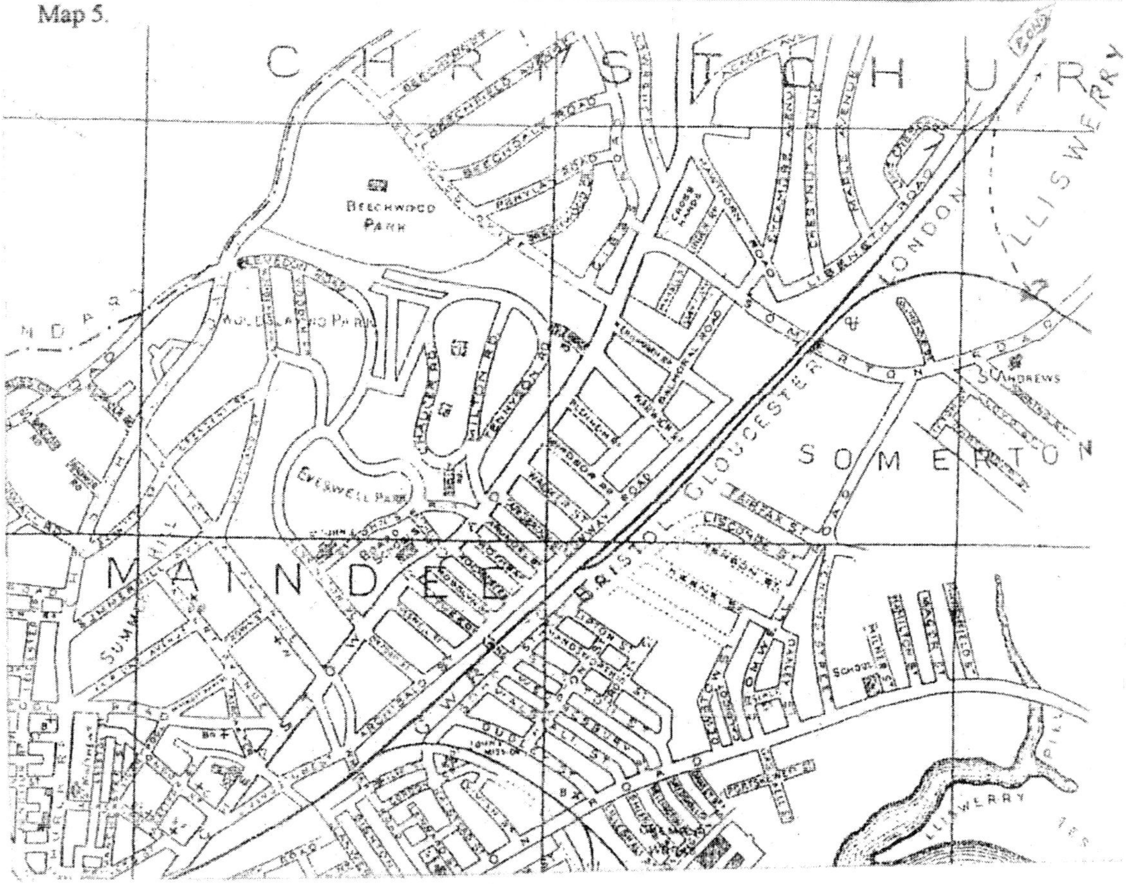

Changing Times.

<u>Map 4: 1901</u>. Canals and coal gave way to steam and steel. Logan and Renny, the canal engineers, sold their farms after the construction of Newport's Transporter Bridge. It was built to convey the town's workforce across the river, to the new Steel Company that had been built on a large plot of land just beyond Somerton Farm. (Lesson 25) – The bridge: A Grade 1 listed building, is still in perfect working order and celebrated its centenary in August 2006

<u>Map 5:</u> Housing now extended to the north boundary. Rennie's Pen-y-lan Park, replaced by tree named roads. 'Maindee Mansion' was demolished and Somerton Farm replaced by streets bearing the names of towns from which job seekers had travelled to live near the steel works.

After roads had been laid on the sites of 'Maindee Park' and 'Maindee Hall', the building programme to be know as Poets' Corner was interrupted by the Great War.   However as a result of Eveswell being bombed during the 2nd World War the building programme was completed.

Those who had lost home and loved ones formed one of the first self-build groups in Britain. They requested land from the town council. Their wishes granted, the would be residents worked as a team, pooling their time and skills to build homes, each on their alloted plot.

The scenery has changed, yet traces of the 19th Century can still be seen – as Big Brown Rabbit observed when visiting the 21st Century... From time to time. (Lesson 28.)

Beechwood House was damaged by fire - yet has undergone restoration to stand majestically again, amidst the trees of Beechwood Park, overlooking the ravine, stream and strange drain that took Hop-pity time travelling to Somerton Pond – now known as Lliswerry Pond - a short distance from Newport's Wetland Centre... The once virgin countryside – today a City's Centre!

The old town boundary that crossed the Usk in the 19th Century, has since taken a leisurely stroll along another riverbank. Where feeling rather tired it sits on the riverside at the 2nd Severn Bridge Crossing, waiting to welcome you to the golden land of dragons and daffodils.

-:-:-

Billy the Kid (1859 - 1882) at age twenty-two had killed 21 men... (Wanted Posters - Lesson 16)

Charles Darwin (1808 – 1882) who wrote 'Origin of The Species' -1848 -'52... (Ref. Lesson25).

-:-

ISBN 142510255-7

Edwards Brothers Malloy
Thorofare, NJ USA
November 18, 2013